W9-BRT-215

Captain John Murdock, USMC, Retired, with the strong hands and gruff sarcasm, was all male, all muscle and a mystery to her.

Maggie's mind replayed every moment of that encounter with her new neighbor. She could still hear the deep voice demanding she do the right thing despite her fears—still feel the big hands that had accidentally warmed her and made her feel unexpectedly secure when he'd clasped her fingers. She could easily recall her gratitude that he'd spoken kindly to her chatty son even though she'd done nothing to encourage any type of conversation. John Murdock was bigger and stronger than her in every way.

She should be afraid of a man like that.

And yet she'd run to him for answers and assurances.

But blindly trusting a man like that was a mistake she couldn't afford to repeat. Was she a fool to believe the military cut of his golden-brown hair and proud carriage of his shoulders meant he was a man who'd defend her?

JULIE MILLER

THE MARINE NEXT DOOR

Harlequin®

TORONTO NEW YORK LONDON
AMSTERDAM PARIS SYDNEY HAMBURG
STOCKHOLM ATHENS TOKYO MILAN MADRID
PRAGUE WARSAW BUDAPEST AUCKLAND

ISBN-13: 978-0-373-69617-8

THE MARINE NEXT DOOR

Copyright © 2012 by Julie Miller

ABOUT THE AUTHOR

Julie Miller attributes her passion for writing romance to all those fairy tales she read growing up, and to shyness. Encouragement from her family to write down all those feelings she couldn't express became a love for the written word. She gets continued support from her fellow members of the Prairieland Romance Writers, where she serves as the resident "grammar goddess." This award-winning author and teacher has published several paranormal romances. Inspired by the likes of Agatha Christie and Encyclopedia Brown, Ms. Miller believes the only thing better than a good mystery is a good romance.

Born and raised in Missouri, she now lives in Nebraska with her husband, son and smiling guard dog, Maxie. Write to Julie at P.O. Box 5162, Grand Island, NE 68802-5162.

Books by Julie Miller

HARLEQUIN INTRIGUE

*The Precinct
**The Precinct: Vice Squad
‡The Precinct: Brotherhood of the Badge
‡‡The Precinct: SWAT
***The Precinct: Task Force

CAST OF CHARACTERS

Maggie Wheeler—This KCPD desk sergeant and single mom is ready to make detective. Volunteering for the Rose Red Rapist Task Force is a smart career move. A rape survivor herself, she doesn't need the threats and violence from her past, or a brooding new neighbor, to interfere just as she's ready to finally move forward with her life.

John Murdock—Just home from an eighteen-month stint in a war zone with his marine corps reserves unit. This once-gentle giant is struggling to adjust to normal life again. But there's nothing normal about the threat stalking the leggy redhead in the apartment next to his. Can he tame his own demons long enough to save her and her young son?

Travis Wheeler—Maggie's ten-year-old son. Nuts about baseball and determined to protect his mom.

Danny Wheeler—Maggie's ex has a prison record. And a temper.

Lawrence Boyle—An old friend of Danny's, who gives him a job as an exterminator.

Joe Standage—The super at the Corsican Apartment Building where Maggie and John live.

Gabriel Knight—Reporter covering the investigation—and the task force's frustrating lack of success.

Dean Murphy—A firefighter at Station No. 23.

Miss Applebaum, Bernard Cutlass and the Wongs—The mysterious neighbors on the seventh floor.

The Rose Red Rapist—He hasn't stalked a woman in Kansas City for years now. But he's back.

Prologue

"Maybe there won't be a wedding!"

"How can you say that?"

Hidden by the trash bins where he'd been working after regular customer hours, the man lingered in the shadows outside the Fairy Tale Bridal Shop near downtown Kansas City and watched as the back door swung open and the young couple stormed out into the parking lot.

An older woman, her hair gleaming like brass in the illumination of the trendy neighborhood's wrought-iron lights, hurried after them. "You ungrateful little girl."

"Please." The shopkeeper following behind her tried to intervene but wasn't assertive enough to be paid any heed. "You shouldn't be making big decisions right now—"

"No, Mother." The young woman whirled around and he caught his breath. She was so classically beautiful. So perfect. So like… *No, don't go there.* "It's young *woman. Grown* woman. Not *little girl.* You can't force this on me. It's too big. Too much. I don't want this."

"You still want *me*, right?" The tall man in the tailored suit reached for her.

She shrugged off his touch with an unladylike grunt and no answer.

"Sweetheart." The tall man smiled and clasped his hands around her shoulders, trying to soothe her temper.

"Let's go to our dinner reservation and use the time to cool off. It's been a long day."

"I'm not hungry." She shook him off.

The man in the shadows smiled beneath the mask he wore over his nose and mouth. That one had fire. An insidious awareness of her feminine strength licked through his veins and made him clench his fist around the bag he carried.

"Then let me drive you home. We'll talk."

"No!" The young beauty spun around and stamped her high heels toward the sidewalk that ran along the street. "I'll catch a cab."

"Sweetheart?"

"She really shouldn't—"

When the young man and mousy shopkeeper moved to follow, the mother stopped them both. "Don't bother. She's been like this for weeks now. I'll try to talk some sense into her when she gets home."

Seriously? They were letting her march off by herself? Not that this was as dangerous a neighborhood as it had once been now that buildings were being renovated and new shops and young professionals were moving in. And the Shamrock Bar just a couple of blocks over, where a good cross-section of KCPD cops liked to hang out after hours, offered some degree of crime deterrence. Still, a woman alone, brave enough to face the city at night—too upset to be truly aware of her surroundings…

The man glanced up. The last vestiges of graying twilight were giving way to stars and a dim crescent moon. Night was falling, and it would be a dark one. Traffic was light between the race of rush hour and the incoming surge of the city's nightlife.

She wouldn't find that cab anytime soon.

The forgettable woman went back into her shop. With

a silent nudge, the bossy mother and groom-to-be climbed into their car.

His pulse raced in anticipation at the opportunity at hand. The shop door locked. The car drove off. It would be so easy. It had been so long.

"Don't." A voice of reason inside his head tried to warn him off the impulse heating his blood. *"You don't need this anymore. You're better than this."*

But he wanted. Hungered.

And she was all alone.

He dropped his bag to unzip his jacket and reach inside his pocket. Everything he needed was in his vehicle. It would be so easy.

"I told you to get rid of those things. Don't think this way. Stop."

But he'd done without for so long, he'd been so good. Still, the rage burned inside him every time he thought of…her.

And the hurt. The humiliation.

It wasn't his fault. She couldn't do this to him. Not again. He wouldn't let her. He needed her to pay. He needed to take back all she'd stolen from him.

"It's not the same. You're confused."

"Shut up," he muttered, feeling his own hot breath moisten the fibers of the mask he wore.

He moved from the shadows to peek around the corner of the brick building. The street was practically empty. Storefronts were dark. The apartments above them were far removed from a world that was quickly shrinking to the quick, purposeful strides of the blonde woman and his own raging need.

Sliding his hand into his pocket, he turned off his phone, in case someone called and distracted him. In case someone thought they could track him down. This was just him and the woman now.

"Stop. She isn't worth it," the voice argued.

But the white-hot haze inside his brain wasn't listening. He ran to his vehicle and started the engine. He looked to the right, to the left, then pulled out of his parking space.

And even though the sun had set, he put on his dark glasses and followed her up the street.

Chapter One

I want to see you.

KCPD desk sergeant Maggie Wheeler had never seen an uglier flower. Not that there was a thing wrong with the cultivated shape and color of the pink spring tulip or the matching ribbon and tall bud vase.

But the florist's card burned her fingertips, and everything the flower that had once been her favorite represented stirred like a swarm of angry bees in her stomach. She breathed a measured sigh between tight lips. Why couldn't the past just stay buried in the past?

If the young man who'd delivered the gift hadn't already disappeared, she'd have sent it back to be delivered to a hospital or nursing home where the tulip and baby's breath could be appreciated. But because that option had left the building, she had no choice but to drop the whole thing into the trash at the end of the counter and empty out the shavings from the front desk pencil sharpener on top of it. She wadded up the card and tossed it in for good measure, too.

"Maggie." Fourth Precinct chief Mitch Taylor tapped the counter as he strode by, then flicked his finger toward the bank of meeting rooms on the far side of the maze of detectives' desks that filled the main floor. "You're with me. Bring your computer and sit in on this meeting."

Maggie shot up to attention, as startled by the order as she was by the interruption. "Me, sir?"

The chief turned and winked, walking backward without slowing his pace. "If you want to see how a task force works, get in here and take notes for me."

"Yes, sir."

She didn't wait to be asked twice.

The flower was forgotten as Maggie grabbed her laptop off her counter, made sure Officer Allen could cover her station at the front desk, and hurried down the hallway after Chief Taylor. She followed him through the door into Interview Room A and quickly slid into the closest empty seat around the long conference table.

She was used to handling odd jobs around the precinct office, but anticipation had her perched on the edge of her chair. Her gun and badge were just as real as the other hardware in the room. And even though her expertise was paper pushing and patience, she was more than ready to move up in both pay scale and prestige at the police department. At thirty-five, she might wind up being the oldest rookie detective on the force, but she'd finally earned her college degree. She was ready to take on investigative work, ready to take the professional rank test and do the interviews to earn her detective's shield. A little casework experience, even vicariously tagging along at the inaugural meeting of KCPD's new major crime task force, would look good on her résumé when she put in for the promotion.

Per the chief's specific request, she'd notified each of the law enforcement professionals gathered here this morning. Detectives. A police psychologist. Uniformed officers like herself. A representative from the crime lab.

You deserve to be here, she reminded herself. It had taken her a long time to feel like she was worthy of anything good or exciting in her life. Sometimes, a new situation like this one could still make her flash back to that awful time when she hadn't believed in herself—when she hadn't even thought she'd survive.

But she believed now. She was here for herself. Here for her ten-year-old son, Travis, and their future. She was in this room because Chief Taylor believed she should be.

Letting those positive thoughts drown out the unsettled worry over the message and flower she'd received, Maggie wiped the perspiration from her palms on the navy twill of her pant leg, steadied her nerves with a quiet breath and opened her laptop. All right, so maybe she was just here as a glorified stenographer to take notes, but her pulse still raced. This was the kind of work she wanted to do. Not just man a desk and be the smiling, efficient, nonthreatening face of KCPD that most citizens saw when they came into the building.

Maggie knew Chief Taylor had a soft spot for her. She'd served in his precinct back when he'd been the newly appointed captain of the first watch. Now he was running the show. She'd lost a little girl, given birth to a son, gotten divorced and worked her butt off to maintain a full-time job to support her child while she'd taken classes to earn the degree her ex had once denied her. The chief understood how badly she wanted that promotion and had no doubt invited her to sit in on this meeting to give her some real experience and a taste of where she wanted her career to go.

She was expecting formal introductions, maybe some kind of pep talk to get them fired up for a particular project. At the very least, she expected Chief Taylor to spell out the new team's purpose and why the commissioner had charged him with the job of selecting a task force for a special investigation.

She wasn't expecting the terse greeting from her barrel-chested boss when he reached the head of the table. "He's back."

He followed up the cryptic pronouncement by slapping a file folder on top of the table.

Even from the opposite end of the room, she could see the crime scene photos that spilled out. She could make out a woman's blond hair and a puffy, bruised face. She could see a lot of crimson on those photographs. Blood.

Nick Fensom, the stocky, dark-haired detective sitting closest to Chief Taylor pulled the folder in front of him and opened it. "The Rose Red Rapist?"

"That's right."

Maggie's stomach knotted beneath her thick leather belt and her gaze darted up to the chief's brown eyes, questioning him. Maybe his invitation to sit in on the meeting hadn't been an impromptu gesture of kindness after all. She'd once been in photos like that.

But Chief Taylor wasn't even looking at her. What if she had a unique understanding of that victim's emotions—shock, betrayal, pain, rage, fear, distrust? That didn't mean the chief had an ulterior motive for inviting her to the meeting. A decade had passed since that horrific time, and she'd put it behind her to focus on the present and future. She was simply overreacting to a gruesome coincidence. She was a cop. A future detective. A fast typist.

Not a sacrificial lamb lured into the room to be probed and profiled by the others at the table. *Get a grip, Sarge.*

Maggie's nostrils flared as she eased the prickly instinct to defend herself on a deep, quiet breath, and dropped her gaze to the screen in front of her. While that feverish impulse to guard against any sort of attack dissipated through the pores of her freckled skin, she concentrated on typing in the names and initial comments of everyone in the room.

Chief Taylor spelled out the details included in the file. "Same M.O. as that unsolved serial rapist case we worked a few years back. Blitz attack. Threat of a weapon once the victim is conscious. None of the victims have been found at the actual scene where the rape occurred, although how they're moved from one place to another isn't always clear. We've got nothing but the vaguest of descriptions of our perp. Male. Tall. There's not even a consensus on his race. He wears gloves and a mask. None of them have seen his face although this most recent victim has some other identifiers that might give us a lead."

"Other identifiers?" Detective Spencer Montgomery, whose short red hair had occasionally earned a question about whether he and Maggie were siblings—other than her son, Maggie had no relatives in the Kansas City area—sat across from his partner, Nick Fensom. Detective Montgomery adjusted his tie and leaned forward. Glancing around the room, she could see he was the senior detective, and his cool and confident demeanor reflected that status. "Such as?"

"His voice."

"Voices can be altered," Montgomery pointed out.

"Smells," the chief countered. "She thought she detected something chemical."

"That's pretty vague." Detective Montgomery wasn't easily convinced.

A dark-haired woman, wearing a CSI windbreaker and sipping something from a stainless-steel travel mug, introduced herself as Annie Hermann, the task force's liaison with the crime lab. "If we can identify the chemical or compound the vic smelled, then that could be a significant clue. It might give us the perp's profession or a medical condition. Or tell us something about his vehicle."

Detective Fensom shot CSI Hermann a look across the table and shook his head. "The perp leaves a red rose with each of his vics. It's probably fertilizer or preservative from the florist's shop."

The petite Annie Hermann straightened in her chair. "Then maybe he works with flowers. The back of a florist's van would be the perfect place to hide a body. The lab is running tests right now to isolate and eliminate any chemicals absorbed by the rose."

Maggie continued to type. Analyzing a rose? Would an analysis of the tulip she'd just trashed reveal the motive behind the anonymous gift? Not that she had any doubt as to the sender and the seeming innocence of his request.

"It's a viable clue," Annie Hermann insisted.

"We'll see." Detective Fensom rocked back in his chair, unconvinced.

The CSI poked the tabletop with her finger. "Science gives us facts. It eliminates false leads and solves cases."

"Not without any context to put those facts in. Cops solve cases. I'll bet my gut has led to more arrests than your science."

"Back to your corners, you two." Chief Taylor silenced the debate. "The perp's smell isn't much to go on, but it's a lead. Hermann, I want you to follow up on it." He turned to the dark-haired detective. "And, Nick, I want you to use that gut to lead you to anyone on the streets who can tell us about this guy or these abductions. Anything is more than we've got right now."

"Yes, sir, Chief."

"Yes, sir."

As the detective and the CSI settled back in their chairs, Maggie typed in the information, ignoring the crawl of memories over her skin beneath her uniform. Smell was indeed a vivid identifier because it left such an impression on the senses. Some of the most indelible memories she had from that hellish weekend her ex had gone off the deep end were of the smells—blood, booze, smoke, sweat—and the flowers he'd given her afterward. And to this day she would not use scented fabric softener or scented detergent in the laundry because of the memories that particular fresh smell evoked.

She nodded in silent approval of the victim's power of observation. If she could identify her attacker by whatever scent was uniquely his, then the task force had a good shot at nailing him.

Provided they could catch him first.

Detective Fensom grumbled as he gathered up the photos. "What's with the rose, anyway? It's as though he thinks that hint of romance makes it an act of passion instead of violence." He shoved the folder onto the blond woman in an elegant suit sitting beside him.

Dr. Kate Kilpatrick was more interested in skimming through the transcript of the report from the investigators who'd originally handled the case. Although Maggie had received counseling from the police psychologist years earlier, she'd never known Dr. Kilpatrick to work actively on an investigation before. "Maybe it's a sign of remorse?"

"More like a sick memorial for everything he's taken from her." Edison Taylor was the only other uniformed officer at the table. But the patch on the short sleeve encircling his biceps indicated he was a specially trained K-9 cop. "I thought he was off the streets, Uncle Mitch. What's it been? Eight—"

"Ten years, Pike," the chief answered, using a nickname that Maggie knew referred to the surname Edison had before he'd been adopted into the Taylor family as a young teen. "Either he went away to prison for some other crime and now he's back on the streets, or we've got us a nasty copycat."

"So why exactly am I here?" Pike asked. "I'm not an investigator, a profiler or a lab tech."

"I'm counting on you and your unit to provide extra security around the crime scenes. Run searches for us and so on."

Dr. Kilpatrick nodded. "Everything I've read so far on the case indicates our perp is someone who blends into the community well. His victims appear to be unfortunate targets of opportunity. Yet no one seems to notice anything suspicious, much less feel threatened, before the attacks. It would make sense that he'd also be around after the fact, perhaps reliving the assault by watching the neighborhood and police response to his crimes."

"Flying under the radar the entire time," Chief Taylor continued. "The commissioner and I agree that stepping up patrols all across the city might drive our perp underground and create an unnecessary panic. If this is the same guy from before, he'll stick to a part of Kansas City he knows. I want to narrow down the area where he hunts for his victims and use your unit and the dogs to keep a close watch in the neighborhood where he's most likely to strike again."

"And that would be?"

"Right now we're looking at Irish Town and the City Market district. There are a lot of new businesses, renovated offices and apartment buildings there. Plenty of women live or work there, or travel in and out to shop and socialize. That's where he abducted his latest victim." He circled the table to scan the file for the info he needed. "She was abducted just after an appointment at the Fairy Tale Bridal Shop."

"I know the area well enough." The blue-eyed officer reached down and scratched between the ears of the muscular German shepherd stretched out at his feet. "Hans and I will be ready."

Mitch Taylor returned to his chair at the head of the table. "Maggie?"

"Sir?" She snapped to when the chief called her name, forcing herself to interact instead of just recording information.

"I want you on the computer getting me the name of every violent offender whose prison term fits the time frame for when our perp was missing in action. The conviction doesn't have to be rape. Look for physical assaults, armed robberies."

"Specifically, crimes against women," Dr. Kilpatrick clarified. "This guy is all about power. Either he's punishing his victims for some perceived wrong done to him by a woman, or he's compensating for a real or self-perceived weakness—and women are easier for him to control. He feels stronger, more masculine, by putting someone else down."

"He could just be some sexual deviant nut job," Fensom groused.

"Possibly," the doctor conceded. "As I recall, there's no real pattern to his victim type. He's assaulted a Black woman, an Asian, blondes, brunettes. There has to be something that ties these women together—that makes them his type."

Okay, support. Tech support. Maggie wasn't the best-trained person when it came to researching through the KCPD database, but she was a fast learner. "I can do that. Look for men recently released from prison convicted of crimes against women."

She could already name at least one suspect who fit the

description without typing in a single keystroke. And she'd tossed his gift into the trash.

Annie Hermann had a different idea. "You know, some sickos can suppress their urges for a while. Or maybe the crimes just haven't been reported."

Despite the subtle tension between Annie and Detective Fensom, the chief thought her idea had merit. "It's possible he took his game to some other town and now he's back."

Maggie raised her gaze to the chief's and put forth an idea of her own. "I'll access the FBI's database and run a nationwide scan for any reports that match our perp's M.O."

"Better make that international," Spencer Montgomery suggested. "Our guy could have been way off the grid."

Maggie opened up a note pad on her screen and jotted down the task. She scooted the case file with the haunting photos around the table while she typed.

Chief Taylor pulled back the front of his suit jacket and propped his hands at his waist. "I know all the scenarios to explain why he's back in KC, doing this sick stuff to women. I want to know how we stop him."

"Is this…" Annie set down her drink and pulled an 8 x 10 of the latest victim from the file.

"Bailey Austin." Spencer Montgomery plucked the photo from her hand, perhaps looking at it a little longer than necessary for simple identification before picking up the folder and sliding it back inside. But he was a hard man to read, and maybe Maggie had only imagined the hesitation regarding the victim's picture. "It doesn't help that his first victim out of the block is the stepdaughter of one of the wealthiest men in Kansas City. Her stepdaddy, Jackson Mayweather, will do whatever it takes to protect his family. That could generate a lot of press we don't want."

"And makes us look bad that he's still on the street," his partner added. "That has to feed this perp's power trip."

Chief Taylor nodded. "I've already gotten a call this morning from Mr. Mayweather, after he talked to the commissioner. He's agreed to use discretion and defer to us, at least until we get our investigation under way."

"Is Miss Austin okay?" Montgomery asked.

"Look at the pictures," Annie said. "She was brutalized."

"I'm asking, did she survive? Is she alive? Coherent?" Maybe Maggie had only imagined an emotional reaction from Detective Montgomery because he cleared his throat and his tone became every bit as clipped and clinical as a scientist discussing his research. "I'd like to question her—as soon as Dr. Kilpatrick here thinks she can handle it. If we can't talk to a suspect, the next best thing is talking with the vic. If we could get a grasp on what she was thinking and doing that made her pop up as a target for this bastard, that might give us a lead to track him down."

Dr. Kilpatrick held the detective's gaze across the table. "I'd suggest sending an interrogator with a little more tact and compassion than you, Spencer."

"I get the job done," he argued.

The police psychologist was unfazed by the chill in his tone. "Whoever interviews the women who were attacked needs to understand their victimology. Rape victims require an intuition, an empathy, even, to get them to communicate. You may be dealing with anger, extreme distrust, fear of reprisals. They could be shut down and unreachable. Research indicates that some women even feel they deserved the attack, and won't cooperate with police to catch their rapist."

Nick Fensom swore beneath his breath. "Nobody deserves what happened to her."

Kate Kilpatrick nodded. "Unless you've been through that, though, it's difficult to understand the victimology."

The letter *k* repeated in row after row on the computer screen as Maggie's fingers stilled on her keyboard. Chief Taylor hadn't asked her into the meeting just to take notes after all. She was certain of it.

Detectives, a police psychologist, a crime lab liaison and a security expert. Their presence on the task force made sense. Now she understood that her presence here made sense, too.

Maggie knew what it was like to be a rape victim better than anyone else sitting at this table, as far as she was aware. She'd long ago locked down that part of her life and moved on the best she could to raise her son and provide a healthy, normal existence for them both. But if she could help Bailey Austin recover from her attack—if she could get the other victims to talk or offer some unique insight that could prevent the Rose Red Rapist from striking again…then maybe it was time to for her to unlock that terrible expertise.

Her attacker had been a free man for precisely forty-three days now. And even though a court order legally prevented Maggie from ever having to deal with her ex-husband again, she'd awakened every morning and fallen asleep each night for the past forty-three days, wondering if this was the day Danny Wheeler would return and finish what he'd started ten years earlier. The tulip this morning told her she'd been right to worry. She knew how frightened Bailey Austin was feeling right now—how wary and exposed and unable to trust she'd be until the bastard who'd raped her was put behind bars.

Maggie Wheeler understood victimology. Chief Taylor was a smarter man than he sometimes let on. He'd known exactly what he was doing when he'd asked her to join this meeting. Some favor.

"I'll let you all work out the details." He was wrapping up the meeting. "Montgomery's running this show, but I want a daily report. Anything you need, don't wait and go through channels if there's any kind of delay. You need a warrant, you need to talk to another division, you need access to sealed records—whatever it might be—you come to me and I'll expedite the request. As of now, this investigation is priority one." Maggie deleted all the extra letters and saved her notes, working up the courage to raise her hand and interrupt. "I have a wife and a daughter. I want this bastard off the streets."

The answering chorus of "Yes, sirs" told her the meeting had ended. People were breaking into smaller discussions. Pike Taylor urged his dog to its feet. The chief opened the door and was leaving the room.

Do it. Ten years of recovery and a hard-won independence urged Maggie to rise to her feet. One gift from her ex wasn't going to intimidate her into sitting on her hands and allowing another woman to be hurt. She had a unique skill that no one else in this room could bring to the table. She breathed in deeply and made her decision. Men like her ex-husband and the Rose Red Rapist didn't get to terrorize the women of Kansas City. Not when she could do something to help stop them.

"Do it," she whispered to herself, closing her laptop and hurrying after Chief Taylor. She caught up to him in the hallway just outside his executive assistant's office. "Chief, could I talk to you a minute?"

He pulled back his sleeve and checked his watch before offering her half a smile. "I was hoping I'd pique your interest." He nodded to the woman at the desk in his outer office as he ushered Maggie through to his office. "Brooke, hold my calls."

"Right, Mitch." Brooke Kincaid, probably Maggie's best friend here at Fourth Precinct headquarters, mouthed a question to Maggie. *Are you okay?*

Maggie nodded, trading a thumbs-up sign with her friend, even though she was certain she looked pale as a ghost. She had to do this. She needed to be a part of this team.

Chief Taylor closed his office door and gestured to a seat on the near side of his massive walnut desk. "I know you don't have investigative experience yet, Maggie. But I also know how much you want to make detective. I hate to lose the efficiency you bring to running the front desk, but I think you could be an asset to the team. You'd be invaluable talking to the victims." His leather chair creaked as it took his weight. "I don't want to force you because I know it's a personal subject for you, but—"

"You don't have to give me a sales speech, sir," Maggie assured him. "You know my history with Danny. And I know that's why you asked me to join that meeting."

A much younger Mitch Taylor had been the arresting officer when her ex had finally answered for his violence against her. "I didn't want to give you too much time to think about it. I figured you might talk yourself out of helping."

"If you want someone who understands the victimology of the women the Rose Red Rapist preys on, I'm… qualified."

"You're sure? This could bring up some painful memories." He braced his elbows on the desk and leaned toward her. "And I won't lie to you—Danny has been out of prison a couple of months now, hasn't he? This has to be a particularly trying time for you. Nothing about this investigation will be easy."

She should have known a cop as experienced and on-the-ball as Mitch Taylor would be aware of her ex-husband's release from prison. Maybe he even considered her ex a person of interest because Danny Wheeler's time locked up in Jefferson City roughly matched the gap in the Rose Red Rapist attacks. She didn't know whether Danny would target any other woman except her, but then she hadn't known the extent of the violence he was capable of when she'd married him either.

"I want to do this, Mitch." This was her chance to prove to Chief Taylor that she was not only ready, but that she also deserved to make detective. It was also her chance to prove to herself that she truly had moved beyond the past that had once shadowed every aspect of her life. She was a fighter. A mother. A cop. A college graduate. She was nobody's victim anymore. "Some things, no matter how difficult they are, are worth doing. I want to fight for these women—be their advocate if I can. I want to join your task force."

Chapter Two

This was getting old.

John Murdock's thick arms and thighs flexed easily as he lifted two more boxes of books from the back of his pickup and shut the tailgate. But his right knee ached, and shards of phantom pain radiated down into his ankle and foot. He'd been at this all day—long enough for the sun to go down outside—packing, carrying, unpacking, hauling some more. Even though he'd made the trip several times already without incident, habit had him checking the cars on either side of him, and behind each crumbling brick-encased support pillar as he limped across the cracked concrete of the parking garage below his building.

He wondered how long the pain that wasn't really there would stay with him—possibly the rest of his life according to many of the doctors and therapists who'd worked on him. He wondered how long it would take before it stopped feeling like he was just going through the motions expected of him by *civilized* society, and he truly felt like he was home. He was getting used to the quizzical looks from strangers, setting him apart because they viewed him as some kind of hero or they felt sorry for him. Either option set his teeth on edge and made it hard to interact without second-guessing every word or gesture directed his way.

He wondered when he'd feel like celebrating surviving

his last tour of duty in Afghanistan, when he'd feel like unpacking his Purple Heart, Silver Star and other medals and deployment ribbons. He wondered when he'd be ready for a beer with old friends or facing the job—and the woman he loved but could never have—that he'd left behind. It didn't matter that he'd lived his whole life in Kansas City before reupping with the Corps. He felt like a stranger in his own town, with his own things, inside his own skin.

He'd left a part of himself behind on that roadside in Afghanistan. In more ways than one.

Returning to the Corps was supposed to have been a fresh start for him—coming home after his stint was up, the beginning of a brand-new chapter in his life. Yet he felt stuck, like nothing had changed. He'd loved the wrong woman, raised a sister who no longer needed him, given his spleen and a good part of his right leg, a couple of friends and half of his soul to the enemy he'd gone to fight.

Inside, he was still a long way from coming home.

Adding boxes of books and kitchen supplies, along with a few civilian clothes, to the boring beige of his furnished apartment didn't do much to make this feel like a homecoming. But it got him out of the spare bedroom at his sister's place so she could sell it and get on with marrying her fiancé. And, it was mindless exercise that tired him out and didn't require much thought. Right now it was enough to feel less like a burden and to look forward to a decent night's sleep.

John slowed when he heard footsteps ahead of him. Two sets of footfalls on the far side of that last pillar. He was a big enough man that it'd take a pretty bold mugger to come after him. But size alone wasn't a deterrent if the perps were hyped up on some kind of drug or they took a closer look at his disability and mistook him for an easy mark—if there was a mugger at all.

Running into normal, everyday people who expected normal, everyday conversation out of him was almost more daunting than facing someone who wanted to hurt him. He'd been in survival mode for over a year now, and adjusting to *normal* was taking just as long as the psychologist who'd debriefed him when he'd mustered out had said it would.

The curve of a butt in navy blue slacks disappearing between the open doors of the garage's elevator almost made him stop in his tracks as he rounded the last pillar and passed the wall of junction boxes and access panels and fire emergency equipment. So the challenge would be normal, everyday civility if he got on that elevator. Would the woman who owned those curves notice the empty pant leg? Or the carbon-fiber composite rod sticking out of his boot? Would there be a slew of curious questions or politely stilted silence as she avoided eye contact with him? Maybe she'd just stare at the scars on his neck, arm and hand. A vein ticked along the column of his throat as the relative tranquility of being alone warred with his common sense.

Who knew how long he'd have to stand there holding the heavy boxes before his ride returned again? The Corsican might be rich in architectural history and renovation potential, but the building had just the one elevator that ran to all ten floors. He might as well start dealing with *normal, everyday* now rather than putting it off indefinitely.

"Hold the elevator," he called out, lengthening his stride.

The woman gasped. Maybe he'd just startled her. "Hurry up," she muttered—to her companion.

John bristled at the whispered slight. Were they trying to get away? Maybe she'd gotten a glimpse of him as well and wasn't thrilled about the idea of sharing the tiny space with him either. But if he could make the effort to be civil, then the woman attached to that backside could damn well do the same.

"Hold it," he ordered in a sharper tone. He heard a *"Mom,"* and then a slender, tanned arm shot out to catch the door as he slipped inside. He looked straight into a pair of emerald-green eyes, silently telling the woman that he knew she'd tried to leave him behind. "Thanks."

But when the doors closed and John retreated to the opposite corner to rest his boxes on the railing, he wondered if he'd made a tactical error. That verdant gaze, sparkling with defiance or warning or some other kind of intense emotion, followed him all the way to the back of the elevator before the woman blinked and turned away. Seeing her adjust her stance to position herself between him and the chestnut-haired boy with her made John wish he'd waited for the next ride up after all. *Nice to meet you, too.* He felt her wariness of him like a punch in the gut.

And he'd been worried about making small talk.

This woman meant business when it came to protecting her son from the big, bad strangers of the world. Despite the copper-colored hair twisted up in a bun at the nape of her neck, with a dozen fiery gold wisps popping loose to curl against her skin, she was no dainty female. She was tall, standing nearly six feet, judging by the mere five or six inches John topped her by when he normally towered over most women. She was in uniform and she was armed.

One hand rested on the butt of the GLOCK 9 mm holstered at her waist as she inched closer to the boy who was peeking at him from beneath the bill of his Royals baseball cap. John was pretty sure the protective-mama move was intentional when she turned so he could clearly see the

KCPD badge hanging from the chain beneath her starched collar.

"What floor?" she asked politely enough. But her green eyes darted as though they were assessing his height and width and the distance between them.

"Seventh."

"Travis." She squeezed the boy's shoulder beside the backpack he wore, drawing John's attention to the fact that her skin wasn't tanned so much as it was dotted with hundreds of freckles.

The boy, whom John put in the nine- to ten-year-old range, slipped his ball glove over the handle of the bat he carried before pushing the button and then twisting from his mother's grasp. "Do you live on the seventh floor?"

Well, at least someone in this elevator didn't think he was the spawn of the devil. "That's why I'm going there."

"We just came from baseball practice," the boy announced. "I play in the outfield, but I want to be the second baseman or shortstop. Do you like baseball?"

"Trav." The redhead chided her son in a soft tone that belied her tough-chick image. "What did I say about bothering people?"

"He's no bother, ma'am." Now where did that reassurance come from? He should have been happy she didn't want to talk to him.

The boy named Travis tilted his face up to John's, giving him a clear look at the inherited freckles sprinkled across his nose and cheeks. "I'm not supposed to talk to strangers, but Mom says I need to know all the neighbors on our floor in case she's not home and I need to go to a safe place. We're on the seventh, too. I'm Travis Wheeler."

Safe place? Although there were other eighty-year-old buildings on this block that were in the process of being reclaimed like this one, one of the reasons John had chosen this particular neighborhood was so that his sister could stop in for a visit whenever she wanted to. The fact that Miranda Murdock was a cop, like this woman, didn't matter. Big brothers looked out for their little sisters—even if she was engaged to a man who was just as protective of her as John.

This building was safe. The remodeled structure now surpassed fire codes and he'd been assured by the landlord that retired tenants and young professionals—not gnarly devil men who terrorized women and children—populated the place.

"I'm Captain—" *normal,* civilian *conversation, remember?* "—John Murdock. I work for the Kansas City Fire Department. Out of Station 23."

"You're a firefighter? Cool."

"Sorry." Mama clasped her hand over Travis's shoulder and pulled him back to her without sharing her name and completing the introductions. "You're new here?"

"Yes, ma'am. I've been deployed overseas or stationed in the DC area for a couple of years now. Moving in today." There he went, making a rusty effort to put her at ease.

"What apartment?"

"709."

"Mom, that's right next door to us."

"So it is." The smile for her son faded when she faced John again. "Don't worry, I'm not looking for babysitters. Travis won't be stopping by."

"I'm not a baby—"

"If he needs to—"

"He won't." John almost grinned at Travis's frustrated groan when his overprotective mama hugged her arm across his chest. "There are plenty of other tenants in the building we tru—"

Her gaze wavered and dropped to the middle of

John's dusty gray-green T-shirt where she could read the letters *USMC*.

Trust?

Yep, no need to worry about polite civility with this woman. He was free to be his moody, isolated self, as far as she was concerned.

So why did it bother him that she turned away to watch the buttons for each floor light up without making direct eye contact with him again?

"Can you play baseball with your leg like that?"

"Travis!"

Mama put her fingers over her son's mouth and John finally got the silence he'd thought he wanted until the elevator jerked, an alarm bell rang, and the whole car jolted to an unexpected stop. The redhead yelped as she tumbled into the back wall, but she caught her son and clung to the railing with a white-knuckled intensity, keeping both of them upright.

"What the hell?" John swayed on his feet, but the boxes anchored him into place. The light for the seventh floor was lit up above the door, but the doors didn't open. Beneath the blare of the alarm he listened for any sounds of cables and pulleys reengaging. He reached across the elevator and pounded the alarm button with his fist until it shut off. He tilted his face toward the trap door and machine works above them. Silence. Almost like the building's electricity had suddenly shut off. But why were the lights in the car still on if there was no power to the rest of the elevator? They were good and stuck. So much for life returning to normal. His gaze zeroed in on the ashen skin of the policewoman. "Does this happen often here?"

"Mom?" The kid tugged on the sleeve of his mother's uniform. A worried frown veed between the boy's eyes as he turned to John. "She's got a thing about elevators. She doesn't really like them."

"That's nonsense. I'm fine, sweetie." She cupped her son's face and flashed a smile for his benefit. But John wasn't buying it. Freckles there definitely had a phobia about something. Being trapped? Closed-in places? Fear of falling? "I've never gotten stuck in the elevator here before. But it's an old building. Stuff happens."

"It didn't happen on any of my other rides up and down from the garage."

Her glare told John that she didn't appreciate his pointing out that fact. "We just have to notify the super, Mr. Standage, that we're stuck, and he'll get things moving in no time." Assuming an air of nonchalance, probably to reassure the boy, she crossed to the rows of buttons and opened the emergency phone panel. Only, instead of pulling out the telephone, she dropped down in front of the opening. "There's no phone in here."

"What?"

"It's gone. There's nothing but wires."

"Let me see." John set the boxes of books on the floor and knelt in front of the panel beside her. He'd seen billiard balls ricochet across a pool table slower than the woman shot to the opposite corner of the car, pulling her son with her. So maybe *he* was what she was afraid of.

That didn't bode well for her staying calm in this crisis.

Drawing on years of training to keep victims or locals calm during a rescue attempt with KCFD or raid on insurgents overseas, John pushed aside any insult or guilt he might feel at her obvious aversion to him, and kept his voice as calm as he could make it. It was a little harder to control the jerky movements that might startle her as he pushed to his feet and locked his bum leg into place.

But the woman was wearing a KCPD uniform with sergeant's stripes on the sleeve. There had to be some training that she could draw on, too. "You have a cell phone on you, Sarge?"

"Yes."

He remained by the door and simply spoke over the jut of his shoulder to her. "If you've got Standage's number, call him directly. If not, call 9-1-1 and ask for the fire department. They'll know how to deal with elevator emergencies."

She pulled her phone from the bag looped over her shoulder and opened it to make the call. Good. "You said you were with the fire department now. Do *you* know how to get us out of here?"

"We'll find out what I can remember."

John wedged his big fingers into the slit between the doors. He grunted with the strain on his forearms and biceps until he created a gap wide enough to slide his hands in all the way and get a better grip. "Let's see where we are."

"Joe? This is Maggie Wheeler from 707. We're stuck on the elevator. Are you working on the wiring? Or did the power get cut somehow? Yes. There are three of us."

Once he could get his shoulders and body weight into it, John pushed the doors all the way open and took a step back to assess the concrete wall across from his feet. There was a gap about a yard wide at the top that revealed a white number 7 painted on a pair of outside elevator doors.

"Joe says he'll be right up," Maggie reported, stowing her cell phone. "Of course, that means he'll be taking the stairs, and with his arthritis, that could still be a while. Are we between floors?"

"Yeah." John wasn't looking forward to spooking the woman any further, but right now he was a little glad that he'd gotten stuck in the elevator with the flame-haired

Amazon instead of someone more petite. He glanced back to link up with those rich green eyes. "You got a name, Sarge?"

She nodded. "Maggie."

"Maggie, can you reach those doors and help me open them?"

After a moment's hesitation, she stepped up beside him. Good. That was an old trick that still worked apparently. Calling a person by his or her name got them to focus, maybe even trust a little. Giving that person a specific job to do was often the easiest way to distract her from her fears.

Even though he felt her flinch when their hands brushed against each other, she didn't hesitate to slide her fingers between the doors and help pull them apart. Now they were looking out onto the carpeted hallway of the seventh floor. Weird. The only time he'd seen an elevator not align with the exterior doors was when the power had been deliberately cut by firefighters battling a blaze.

John glanced up. But the damn light for the seventh floor was still lit up. He wouldn't be able to see out into the hallway if the lights were off there, too. What kind of crazy wiring did they have in this place?

"What do we do now?" Sergeant Maggie asked.

John was all for getting off this carnival ride until he could figure out just what the heck was going on. "Son?" He turned back to Travis Wheeler. "Are you a climber?"

"Yes, sir."

"Careful," Maggie warned, understanding what John was asking of her boy. "Shouldn't we wait?"

"Give me the bat and glove first," John instructed. "Backpack, too." The boy handed over his prized possessions and John slid them through the opening onto the eye-level floor above them. "Hold on a sec. So your mama doesn't worry." He met the wary glare of deep green eyes as he picked up the two boxes of books and wedged one against either of the open doors. "That should buy us a few seconds in case anything happens."

"What could happen?" Maggie asked.

John nodded to her purse. "Call Standage back. Tell him not to touch or do anything until we give him the all clear. We don't want the power to suddenly reengage."

While she called the super, John laced his fingers together and bent down to give the boy the boost up he needed.

"Cool, Mom." Travis paused with his fingers and chin resting on the hallway floor. "This is just like that movie I watched at Juan's house. The one where the elevator crashed and almost cut that lady in two when she was climbing out."

"Oh, Lord," came the maternal gasp from behind.

John cringed at the boy's enthusiastic but ill-timed observation and pushed him on through the opening. "Not the time to be talking movies, kid."

As Travis crawled several feet beyond the opening and retrieved his things, John turned to the redhead clinging to the back railing. Without the freckles, there'd be no color to her skin at all. He reached out a hand to her. "Your turn, Sarge."

She clung to the railing. "Joe says he'll wait until I call him again."

"Good, but we're not going to wait. I don't think you want to be stuck in here with me any longer than you have to be."

"You know, it's not really you," she insisted.

"If you say so." But scared was scared, whatever the cause. John's hand never wavered. "Come on, Maggie."

With her eyes locked onto his, her shaky fingers revealing the same distrust, she finally reached out and slid her palm into his. She took a step toward him. "It's been a stressful day. Normally, I'm not a basket case like this. I just…really do have a thing about elevators."

"Fair enough." John pulled her up beside him, then stooped down to create the same step-up with his fingers. "I've decided I've got a thing about this particular elevator myself. There's something wrong with the wiring for parts of it to work and parts of it to stop cold like this. I think I'll be calling KCFD to make an inspection of the place. In the meantime, I say let's get out of here."

"Okay."

She braced one hand on John's shoulder and he lifted her. As she crawled out onto the carpeted floor, she started to slide back and John's hands automatically latched on to…those curves. The flare of her hips and rounded arc of her bottom were an easy grab. And a nice, firm fit.

John swallowed hard and shook his head. He had no grounds to fault the boy for bad timing.

"Sorry," he apologized, giving her a second boost. His hands and eyes had already lingered longer than an impersonal firefighter's should. But the lady cop broke the contact just about as soon as the nerve endings in the tips of his fingers sparked to life at the warmth and suppleness they detected beneath her crisp navy blue trousers.

The view was over and gone within another second, and Sergeant Maggie rolled to safety on the floor above him. John eased a tight breath out between his lips. Something dormant inside him had unexpectedly awakened. Was it just the fact that he hadn't touched a woman for two years? Hugs with his sister and handshakes with doctors and therapists hadn't zinged through him and thrown him off-kilter like this. And prickly redheads had never been his type.

He supposed he should be pleased to discover that life-

threatening injuries and months of recovery hadn't de-
stroyed the baser urges heating his blood right now. But he
was just beginning to get comfortable with being closed-
off and antisocial. Just a few minutes ago, working his
way up to normal civility had been a stretch. And now
he was wondering if that whole sexual lightning bolt had
been a fluke or if he was going to have to curb his natural
instincts to maintain a "just friends" relationship with his
new neighbor.

Busy sorting through his observations and emotions,
and putting them away in various mental compartments,
he was startled to see the long, freckled arm poking back
into the elevator. "Come on," Sergeant Maggie ordered.
"Your turn."

Her tone was much more authoritative and coplike
coming from the free air of the seventh floor than it had
been in the tight confines of the elevator. Intriguing.
Maybe he ought to latch onto that chilly timbre instead of
remembering how she'd filled up his hands if he wanted
to keep a polite distance from her.

He chinned himself up on the edge of the outside door
track, then reached for her hand. With a surprisingly firm
grip, she gave him the extra momentum he needed to hoist
himself out onto the floor. Allowing himself a moment
to catch his breath, John rolled onto his back. "Thanks,
Sarge…"

But the prickly redhead was already slipping her son's
backpack onto his slim shoulders and urging him to their
front door. Nope, he didn't need to worry about hormones
going on alert, being confused about social expectations
of him or trying to be casual friends at all. Sergeant Maggie's quick retreat spoke volumes about how the two of
them were going to get along.

Still lying on the rug, John realized that a nearby

door was propped open and someone with black hair and glasses was peeking out at him. He obliquely wondered if the short, shapeless person was a man or a woman, but there was no mistaking the unblinking curiosity. "Elevator isn't working," he explained. "Welcome to the neighborhood, right?"

The door snapped shut and John laughed at the irony of his worrying about being the antisocial one here on the seventh floor. He sat upright and pushed to his feet. He picked up his boxes from the stalled elevator opening and headed for his apartment. "Yeah, this is one hell of a homecoming, John."

"Excuse me?" the redhead asked.

John shrugged off the polite query. "Nothing, Sarge. Nice to meet you."

Her hesitation spoke volumes. "Nice to meet you, too."

"Hey, Mom. Look."

Great. They were right next door to each other. This could be awkward if the woman preferred him to keep his distance. John shifted his boxes and scooted around mother and son as the boy plucked down a folded piece of white paper that had been tacked to their door.

"Let me see that." Maggie snatched the note from the curious boy's fingers and unfolded it while John fished his keys out of the front pocket of his jeans. "That son of a... This isn't happening. Not now."

"Sarge?"

They both stopped with their keys turned in the locks of their respective doors. The instinctive urge to ask if something was wrong died on John's lips when he saw the color bleed from her cheeks. She stared at the words scribbled on that paper as though hypnotized. Whatever was in that note scared her just as much as the stalled elevator had. Something was definitely wrong.

Not your business, John. She wanted nothing to do with him, her kid asked too many questions and he wasn't looking to make new friends, right?

"Mom?" Travis's fingers touched his mother's arm. "Is it from—?"

"Go inside."

"But—"

"Go." She snapped out of her fixated shock and whisked his cap off his head to press a kiss there before reaching over him to open the door. "There's a snack in the fridge to hold you until dinner."

But Travis, his expression looking oddly mature for one so young, seemed reluctant to leave her. "I was just joking about that movie, Mom. I didn't think you were really going to get cut in half."

John nudged open his own door, giving them some privacy while his neighbor summoned a smile for her son. "I know, sweetie. I know. Wait for me to go through the mail and check the answering machine, though, okay? Now go."

John's muscles were weary with the exertion of the move and their great escape from the elevator as he set the boxes on the carpet. Yet when he turned to close the door, everything in him tensed with guarded apprehension. *She* was there, standing in the open door frame, the note wadded in her left hand while her right hovered near the gun on her hip again.

The warm smile she'd given her son had vanished. "Did you see anyone out here?" she asked. "A man who might have left this note?"

"No." He was vaguely irritated that she seemed to be sizing him up again. Yeah, those green eyes had noticed the fake leg. They swept over the scars. He bristled under her scrutiny. Did she suspect him of tacking the paper to her door? "What's it say?"

"Is this your first trip up from the garage?"

He took a step toward her. This was *his* apartment after all. *She* was the uninvited guest. "My sixth or seventh. What's in the note?"

She braced her feet in an overtly defensive stance and he stopped. What the hell?

John backed up a step and her words came spilling out. "Was there anyone on the elevator with you during any of those trips? Maybe you saw someone in the parking garage you didn't recognize? Was there anyone messing with the wires or controls on that elevator? Or flowers—did you see anyone trying to deliver flowers?" She glanced around at the closed doors behind her. "Sometimes the florist will deliver them to someone else if I'm not at home."

"I didn't see anyone tampering with anything, I don't know anybody here. And I sure as hell didn't get any flowers."

"Did you see a guy with a shaved head and tattoos?"

"I've only met the super, Joe Standage." And the older man wasn't the shaved-head type.

"His hair used to be black. Sometimes he dyes it."

"Joe does?"

"No, my..." Her freckled skin suddenly flooded with heat. Was she embarrassed by her ranting? Intimidated by his unapologetic scrutiny? Alarmed to suddenly realize *she* was the intruder here?

"Is this how you welcome all your new neighbors, Sergeant—" he dropped his gaze to the name badge on her chest pocket, pulled taut by the Kevlar she wore beneath her uniform "—Wheeler? Blow hot, blow cold? Make nice and then freak out? We haven't even been properly introduced."

Whatever this woman's secrets were, she wasn't telling. Instead of answering his accusation, she stuffed the note into her uniform slacks pocket. Then she huffed up in all her warrior Amazon glory, tipping her chin as her skin cooled to peachy dots over alabaster. "I'm Maggie Wheeler. Travis is my son."

"John Murdock."

"Are you military or KCFD?" She eyed the Corps logo on his T-shirt and the jarhead cut that he wore whether he was overseas with his Reserve unit or home in Kansas City, working for the fire department.

"Both. USMC, retired. For about a week now. Moving back to town after my last tour and some rehab. Firefighting is the job I'm coming back to after serving my stint in the Corps." He made another stab at moving closer. "Sarge, um, Maggie…are you okay?"

Her eyes widened as though the question had startled her. Or maybe it was his advance. Before she answered, she retreated into the hallway. "Of course I'm okay. Thank you for serving our country—*Captain* Murdock, was it?"

"Just John now."

She nodded. "I apologize for Travis being so nosy. He's going through a phase where he's completely nuts about baseball and firefighters and…everything. And he's never been shy about speaking his mind." She barely paused for a breath. "I'm sorry I freaked out on the elevator. And the note. It's just that I… Like I said, it was a rough day. Well, you don't need to know that. Welcome to The Corsican, John."

Yep, that sounded sincere.

By the time John reached the door, Maggie Wheeler's was closing. He heard not one, not two, but three separate locks sliding into place.

Something about that message, or the person who'd left it, had his neighbor spooked even more than getting stranded on the elevator had. Even though she wore a gun and a vest and sergeant's stripes, indicating she was no rookie when it came to law enforcement, the woman was spooked.

John narrowed his gaze and looked up and down the hallway. Beyond the super checking him in this morning, and the curious person from the apartment down the hall who hadn't spoken, he hadn't seen a single soul out here all day long. A familiar niggle of unease crept along the back of his neck like when he'd sensed a sniper's rifle focused on him up in the Afghan mountains.

He shook off the hyperawareness and retreated into his apartment. Afghanistan was seven thousand miles away. His years of service were done and he was reporting back to KCFD Station 23 this week to start his new job as an arson investigator assigned to the ladder company with whom he'd once fought fires.

He had plenty on his plate right now to deal with. Leggy redheads and curious kids and somebody else's bad news weren't his concern tonight.

John locked the door behind him and leaned back against it, sweeping his gaze across the beige apartment decorated in wrapped furniture and sealed boxes.

So this was where he was going to live now.

It beat the cot and caves and blood he'd left in the Middle East. It beat the VA hospital and physical therapy units where he'd learned how to walk again.

But with nothing but bare walls and the paranoid lady cop next door, the jury was out on whether he'd call this new place home.

Chapter Three

"I know it's an imposition, but it would be a huge help. Thank you, Coach Hernandez. Yes, I know. Thank you, *Michael,*" Maggie corrected at his insistence. "I'll make it up to you, I promise."

Maggie locked her double-cab pickup and hurried after the other woman and two men striding through the sliding glass doors into St. Luke's Hospital. She'd been working the task force for nearly a week now, and this was the first time she'd been invited to leave the precinct office. If chauffeuring the members of the team was the only way she could get out and do some field work, then a chauffeur she'd be.

"I should be able to pick up Travis after practice this evening. With my new assignment at KCPD, my hours aren't as structured as they used to be, and I just can't get away today to pick him up after school and get him to Little League. But I'll be there by the time you're done."

With an apologetic frown, Maggie nodded to the reception desk volunteer who was pointing to the sign requesting cell phone usage be limited to the lobby and outdoor areas of the hospital. But Michael Hernandez was saying something about his son having Webelo Scouts after practice and that his late wife used to take care of all the transportation stuff anyway, and would Maggie and Travis want to go out to dinner with him and his son afterward? Maggie wasn't finding any polite way to break in to end the conversation with the man she'd asked the favor from.

Seeing Nick Fensom's beefy hand holding the elevator doors open, and withering under the glare from the volunteer, she opted to simply interrupt and wrap up the personal call she'd had to make. "I've got work to do, Coach," she apologized, carefully avoiding using his first name and encouraging anything that might be construed as a personal interest in him. "But I'll call the school to let them know Travis can leave with you. No, I'm quite sure about dinner. I appreciate your help, though. Thanks."

Worried that she'd kept the other task force members waiting, Maggie snapped her phone shut and darted through the open doors to an empty corner of the elevator. As the doors closed, she tried not to make too much of the feeling of déjà vu that skittered along her spine. Was it just last week that she'd gotten stuck on an elevator with her new neighbor, John Murdock? She'd been just as nervous about sharing the tight space with the imposing former marine as she was about joining other members on her first victim interview.

Joe Standage's assertion that he didn't know what the heck was going on in his building, and that he'd have to wait for an expert to help him repair the elevator before it went back into service, was hardly reassuring. Maggie and Travis had gotten into the habit of taking the stairs down to the parking garage anyway, so it wasn't that much of a hardship to use them coming back up, as well. And even though dinner conversations with her son, and her own dreams at night, had centered around the possibility of crashing elevators and being trapped on one with a monster far less interested in helping them escape than John

Murdock had been, Maggie refused to let her fears keep her from doing her job today.

For the trade-off of a free ride this morning, she'd get the chance to observe some of KCPD's best in action. Maggie figured she'd learn more about how to conduct an investigation in one morning by watching the real thing than she'd learned in an entire semester of her interrogation tactics class.

But as the elevator moved upward, it wasn't the anticipation of doing actual field work that had her heart pounding in her ears. Irrational as it might be, sharing an elevator with a man was always a challenge for her. Getting stuck on one was a real nightmare. Perhaps if she'd chosen to take the stairs ten years ago instead of allowing herself to get cornered in the elevator by her enraged husband, she might have gotten away. She might have been spared the attack that had forever changed her life.

She was justified in her aversion to sharing tight spaces with someone bigger and stronger than she was. Even compared to her, standing six feet tall with her work shoes on, John Murdock was an imposing man. Maggie's gaze flickered to the red-haired detective in the tailored suit and tie. Spencer Montgomery was tall, but John Murdock was taller. She looked to the shorter, stockier detective in the black leather jacket. Nick Fensom was broad across the shoulders and muscular, but John was bigger. Not even the artificial leg and obvious limp could lessen the intimidation factor of the unsmiling Goliath who'd moved in next door.

At least, not in her book. Captain John Murdock, USMC, retired, with the strong hands and gruff sarcasm, was all male, all muscle and as much a mystery to her as the handwritten note that still haunted her nights.

Mags—

I miss you. I know I've done you wrong in the past, but I'm a changed man. I've got me a job and I'm not drinking.
I've paid my debt.
When can I see you?
Love,
Danny

Maggie's nostrils flared as she breathed in deeply, willing the frissons of terror still sparking through her system to dissipate so that she could concentrate on the job at hand. The elevator snafu had to be a horrible coincidence that had made Danny Wheeler's note seem that much more threatening. Still, she'd put in a call to her attorney the next morning to discuss getting a new restraining order against her ex-husband. Having the flower delivered to a public building like Fourth Precinct headquarters was easy enough. But how had he found her unlisted address? How had he gotten into the building, past the security gate at the garage and Joe Standage? And why had not one of her neighbors on the seventh floor—whose doors she'd knocked on before some of them were even awake that next morning—seen Danny come and go? Not even those piercing green-gold eyes of John Murdock had seen anyone lurking around her apartment.

Was she living with a bunch of hermits?

Were the tenants in her building too elderly, too foreign, too nearsighted, too hard-of-hearing, too afraid to step up and get involved with their neighbors? If they ever got to know Danny Wheeler the way she did, they'd be smart not to come out of their doors.

But one man had stepped up. Although circumstances

hadn't given him any choice, Captain John Murdock had gotten involved.

As Dr. Kilpatrick and the two detectives discussed their strategy for approaching Bailey Austin, Maggie's mind replayed every moment of that encounter with her new neighbor. She could still hear the deep voice demanding she do the right thing despite her fears—still feel the big hands that had accidentally warmed her backside and made her feel unexpectedly secure when he'd clasped her fingers. She could easily recall her gratitude that he'd spoken kindly to her chatty son even though she'd done nothing to encourage any type of conversation. John Murdock was bigger and stronger than she in every way except for the fact she was armed and had two good legs. She should be supercautious about developing any kind of a relationship with him. She should be afraid of a man like that.

And yet she'd run to him for answers and assurances.

Why had she expected him to be alert to the comings and goings around her apartment, and concerned about her troubles? Yes, he'd stayed calm and gotten her off that elevator when her own fears had kept her from thinking straight. But blindly trusting a man like that was a mistake she couldn't afford to repeat. Did she think his handicap, and the burn scars on his arms and neck from an obviously terrible injury, meant he couldn't harm her? Was she a fool to believe the military cut of his golden-brown hair and proud carriage of his shoulders meant he was a man who'd defend *her?*

Danny had done a stint in the Navy right out of high school. She knew better than to think that just because a man wore a uniform, he was a good guy. She was smarter than that—smart enough to know that outward appearances and little flickerings of awareness in her pulse were no way to judge the true character of a man. She'd fought too hard for her independence to let one panic attack and a lingering curiosity about her mysterious, attractive neighbor keep her from standing on her own two feet.

She would figure out what had gone wrong with the elevator. *She* would find out how Danny had gotten that note to her. *She* would make it clear that he could never be a part of her life, or their son's, ever again. It was what a strong woman would do, what a well-trained KCPD detective would do. This morning she needed to set aside her fascination with John Murdock, and her fears about her ex, to become that detective she wanted to be.

Still, *"Sarge, um, Maggie...are you okay?"*

When was the last time a grown man who wasn't an E.R. doctor or a fellow cop asked her that question?

She knew better than to make anything out of his concern. Heck, they'd barely spoken two words since that night. But it was nice to be asked. Nice that someone was polite enough to notice her distress. Nice to know that wigging out on a man didn't automatically mean he couldn't care. In a neighborly, we-just-survived-a-small-crisis-together kind of caring, of course.

Tamping down the smile that softened her lips, Maggie waited for the other task force members to exit the elevator and get a few steps ahead of her before falling into step behind them.

Bailey Austin's hospital room was easy to spot. It was the one with the John Murdock-sized SWAT cop pacing back and forth in front of the door. She recognized Trip Jones as a coworker who checked in at her desk every morning before the precinct's daily roll-call meeting. His wife was Charlotte Mayweather-Jones, stepsister to the rape victim they'd come to interview. Normally Trip greeted Maggie with a friendly smile.

But there were no smiles for any of them as they approached. "Detective Montgomery. Nick. Dr. Kilpatrick. Sarge." Trip shook hands with each of them. "So this is the new task force?"

"Officer Jones," Spencer acknowledged for all of them. He pulled back the front of his suit jacket to splay his hands at his waist. "How is she?"

Trip shook his head and shrugged. "It's not good. I'm afraid to go in there. I could tell I made her nervous."

"Did she say you remind her of her attacker?" Spencer asked.

"She didn't say anything to me. I guess I can be kind of scary when I'm in the mood to wrap my hands around the neck of the bastard who did this."

Dr. Kilpatrick squeezed his arm in reassurance. "That's an understandable reaction, on both your parts. I'm sure that somewhere inside she appreciates you being here for her."

"Maybe. This family has been through enough with Charlotte's kidnapping, the murder of that worthless stepbrother of hers, and now this. I don't know how much more she can handle."

The blonde psychologist reached for the door handle. "We'll be gentle with her, I promise."

Spencer Montgomery caught the door and followed her in, with his partner right behind them. But when Maggie reached the open door, she stopped. "Wait a minute. We're *all* going in there?"

"We need to question the victim while the incident is still fresh in her mind." Detective Montgomery looked faintly annoyed at having to stop and explain his actions when he faced her.

Maggie shivered with the memory of when *she'd* been the woman lying in that hospital bed. "Her mind's probably still in shock right now. And to see a crowd of armed police officers storm into her room—"

"We're hardly storming," Spencer argued in a hushed tone.

"We're not the bad guys here," Nick Fensom echoed.

Maggie looked over her shoulder to share a rueful glance that included Trip, as well. "Right now, in her mind, pretty much everybody's a bad guy."

A tremulous voice from the other side of the privacy curtain silenced the standoff. "Don't touch me."

Maggie had never met Kansas City socialite Bailey Austin, but she recognized the tenor of a woman fighting to hold on to normalcy and civility, and failing miserably.

A man's voice shushed her. "Sweetie, I'm just so worried—"

"I know."

"This doesn't change how much I love you, how much I want to still marry you. Tell me what you need." Frustration colored his voice. "Anything."

"Bailey, dear, Harper loves you."

"I'm sorry. I just can't… I don't want to talk about the wedding right now, okay?"

"Loretta, dear." That was an older gentleman's voice. Probably Bailey's stepfather.

"No." Loretta Austin-Mayweather's shrill voice took care of any need to be secretive about KCPD's arrival. "I'm going to make everything okay for my daughter. She's going to get married. She's going to have her happily ever after."

"Dear—"

"I just want everything to be the way it was before this happened."

"They're ganging up on her." Maggie whispered the thought out loud.

Nick Fensom's blue eyes narrowed at the observation. "They're family."

"Doesn't matter. They're not listening to what she needs right now."

Spencer was shaking his head as the conversation on the other side of the curtain escalated toward an argument. "We need to talk to her alone if we can. I don't want anybody else's well-intentioned comfort or defense of her to shut her down and keep her from talking, or taint whatever details she can recall."

Nick nodded his agreement. "She may not feel comfortable sharing some of the grittier details in front of her family, anyway."

"Divide and conquer, then." Kate Kilpatrick adjusted her fingers around the strap of her bag and headed for the curtain. She pulled the curtain aside to announce their presence and reveal a tableau of startled friends and family gathered around the bed. "Mrs. Mayweather?" Kate extended her hand to the beautiful blonde woman with the red-rimmed eyes. "I'm Dr. Kilpatrick from KCPD. I'm so sorry this happened to Bailey. As a mother I understand the grief and rage and helplessness you feel at seeing your child harmed." Dr. Kilpatrick had children? She'd never mentioned them. Maggie had never even seen a picture of any family in the psychologist's office. But the moment of surprise passed as the psychologist smoothly manipulated the startled family members. "I have some experience counseling the families of victims. Why don't you and I go out to the lobby and talk for a bit."

Loretta Austin-Mayweather latched on to the sleeve of her husband's suit coat. "I want to be with my baby."

Jackson Mayweather turned his shrewd eyes to Dr. Kilpatrick. "You can calm her down?" The police psychologist nodded, then he patted his wife's hand. "Loretta, I promise we won't go that far. But I think we should talk to the doctor."

Wrapping his arm around his wife's shoulders, the Mayweather patriarch guided her out the door behind the psychologist.

Maggie stepped aside, marveling at the smooth teamwork of the task force members. Nick Fensom said something to Trip's wife, Charlotte, about the red jacket of the certified therapy dog sitting at her feet, and soon the detective was escorting them out the door to join Trip.

But a tall, golden-haired man in a suit maintained his position at Bailey Austin's side. Her fiancé, Harper Pierce, according to an article she'd read in the Kansas City society pages, glared at Detective Montgomery. "You again? Didn't you torment this family enough when you kept harassing us with questions about the Rich Girl Killer?"

"I got the job done, didn't I? We got our man." Spencer's gaze settled for a moment on the bruised face of the young woman in the bed. "We'll get this guy, too."

The one blue eye that wasn't swollen shut blinked open to meet the detective's curiously blank expression. But just as quickly, Bailey closed her eye and turned onto her side, hiding her face toward the blinds at the window.

"You see?" Harper Pierce taunted. "She doesn't want to talk to you."

With his focus squarely back on the hostile fiancé, Detective Montgomery pulled back the front of his jacket, subtly displaying his badge, his gun and his authority to the other man. "You're with me, Pierce. If you truly want to help Miss Austin, that is. Because you were one of the last people to see her that night, I'd like to ask you some questions about the time and events leading up to your fiancée's abduction."

"Bailey needs me here."

"Go." Snatching her shoulder away from Harper's outstretched fingers, Bailey curled into a ball, making it clear that his touch might be the last thing she needed right now. "Please, Harper."

Several moments of silence passed before it fully registered that Maggie was alone in the room with the victim. She shifted on her feet in the shadows beside the door, wondering if she should excuse herself to go observe the interviews or just slip quietly out of the room.

But Bailey Austin's soft voice called to her before Maggie could decide. "You can sit if you want."

Maggie glanced back at the door, then over to the chair and rolling stool beside Bailey's bed. Maybe the young woman was one of those high-society trophy wives-to-be who'd been raised to have impeccable manners—under any circumstance.

But no woman in Bailey Austin's condition needed to be worrying about Maggie Wheeler's feelings right now.

"You need your rest." Maggie thanked her and backed toward the door.

"You don't have to go."

The other woman's voice sounded small, almost devoid of inflection, stopping Maggie's retreat.

She recognized the bleak sound of isolation, the belief that no one could ever truly understand what she'd been through. Maggie's eyes burned with tears of empathy. But she blinked them away, refusing to let another victim feel the utter loneliness and drifting sense of loss she'd endured. Opening up her well-guarded heart, Maggie crossed the room and took a seat on the creaking vinyl stool.

"Your family will be back soon. Or, if you don't want them here, I'm sure your brother-in-law Trip could make that happen." She talked to the gap in the gown between Bailey's shoulder blades. "I'm sorry this happened to you.

You're probably not ready to hear this right now, but I can recommend a victims' group and a therapist who specializes in counseling sexual assault victims."

The younger woman rolled onto her back, turning her puffy face to Maggie. "Were you attacked, too?"

Maggie nodded, going to that matter-of-fact place in her head where she could discuss such things. "January sixteenth—ten years ago."

"I guess it's a date you never forget."

"Haven't yet."

Bailey's bruised blue eye sharpened its focus. "Trip said more detectives who were experts in this kind of crime would be in to question me today. Is that who you guys are?"

Maggie spoke in gentle tones but didn't sugarcoat the truth. "KCPD believes the man who attacked you has raped several women. He disappeared off the radar for a few years, but it seems he's back in Kansas City."

"What he did to me, he did to other women?"

"The M.O.'s match. So our chief has put together a task force." She nodded toward the door. "Detective Montgomery, he's the task force leader. He'll want to ask you some questions when he's done talking to your fiancé."

"I know Spencer." Bailey hugged the blanket covering her up to her chest. "I don't want to talk to him."

She was on a first-name basis with the task force leader? Detective Montgomery had never mentioned a personal connection with the victim. But then, she'd yet to see the man reveal much of anything he didn't want to. "He's one of the best investigators we have."

"I know he is. He helped capture the Rich Girl Killer." But Bailey was sinking beneath the covers, pulling up the blanket like a sheet of armor.

"If there's some kind of problem between you, his partner, Nick Fensom—"

"No."

Maggie released a silent breath and tried again. "Maybe you'd feel more comfortable talking to a woman. Dr. Kilpatrick is a police psychologist, more of an adviser than a cop. She doesn't even carry a gun."

"Why don't you ask me the questions?" Oh, no. Was she serious?

"I'm just support staff. I'm not trained yet—"

"Is it crazy to just want to be left alone?" Bailey's gaze drifted off to a distant corner of the room. "Yet I'm so afraid of being alone now."

"Whatever you're feeling right now is normal." Maggie spoke from practical experience and the stories she'd heard in her support group. "Strangers may make you uncomfortable. For some rape victims, any man can make them nervous. For others, just leaving a familiar place can trigger a panic attack."

Bailey's gaze came back to her. "My sister—well, Charlotte's my stepsister—she was like that. She was kidnapped when she was in high school. For as long as I knew her, she would never leave the house. Until Trip came along. She still doesn't like crowds. And she has a therapy dog to help with the panic attacks." She shifted in the bed to face Maggie. "It took her years to be able to function normally. Is that what I have to look forward to?"

"Surviving a sexual assault is a lot like coping with the death of a loved one. It can affect each victim differently. The length of time it takes to learn how to cope and then move on with your life, and how you get to that point, is different with each person. There's no right or wrong way to recover. And you can't compare your path to anyone else's."

There was a long pause as Bailey processed the answer. Then she surprised Maggie by reaching for her hand. "I never even saw him coming. I was so mad at Harper and my mom, so overwhelmed by all the wedding plans, that I didn't even realize the screeching of brakes I heard in the street was for me."

All of a sudden, Bailey started talking about the attack. Maggie glanced toward the door for help, almost calling out for one of the experts to come back in. But the young woman's grip convulsed around hers with every memory she described. Tears glistened on her bruised cheek and Maggie didn't have the heart to leave her alone or risk her shutting down again.

Maggie thought of her classes, and formulated questions she should ask. But Bailey kept talking. Her eyes were closed, as if replaying events in her mind. "When I woke up, I was in this empty building. On the floor. I mean, on a mattress that was directly on the floor. It was covered in plastic. Everything was."

With one last glance at the door, Maggie gave up on willing reinforcements to arrive. *Do it.* She adjusted her position on the stool, clutched Bailey's hand a little more tightly. If she wanted to be a detective, she might as well start acting like one. "Do you remember anything else about the building? Were you in a small room? A large one?"

"It was sterile."

"You mean it was clean?" The report had mentioned odors she remembered. "Like the hospital?"

Bailey shook her head. "It smelled awful. There was no furniture except for the mattress. No decorations. There were partial walls—framing where walls and windows should go—like a big office or apartment building under construction. Or one being gutted and torn apart, I don't know. Mostly I saw the floor."

"What was the awful smell, do you know?"

"Pickles."

"Pickles?"

"I don't know. I was in and out of consciousness. And he swore he'd cut me or hit me again or put the hood back on me if I so much as spoke." She inhaled a deep breath. "But yeah, now that you say that, it *was* clean—what I could see before he blindfolded me and took me back to that intersection near Fairy Tale Bridal. The plastic underneath me was crystal clear. I remember looking through it and studying the design on the mattress, counting the stitches while he..." Bailey pulled her hand away and rolled onto her opposite side, curling into a ball.

Maggie knew the interview was done and didn't try to push her. "Thank you for talking to me, Miss Austin. I know it's not easy, but knowledge gives us power against this guy. It's the only weapon we have right now to keep anyone else from getting hurt. Thank you for your courage in talking to me."

Curling her fingers into her palm, Maggie fought off the urge to reach out and offer some kind of comfort. But sharing her compassion wasn't why Maggie was here. She'd come to St. Luke's to do her job—or rather, to learn more about how to do her job. Knowing she needed to report this new information about the assault to Detective Montgomery and the others, she adjusted the holster on her belt and stood.

Her fingers were on the door handle when Bailey's soft voice reached her. "Does it get better? Will I ever not hurt? Will I ever feel safe? Will I ever be able to trust again?"

Maggie knew honesty was the only way to answer. "The pain will fade over time." As for the rest? "Like

I said, every survivor's path to healing is different. It'll be tough, but try to remember the important thing, Miss Austin—we survived."

Chapter Four

Just another day at the office, John tried to tell himself as he pulled his pickup into the parking lot next to KCFD Station 23. Although he'd just spent most of his shift down at headquarters, sitting through orientation meetings and filling out paperwork, he knew it wasn't true. The last of his training at HQ was done.

Today was his D-day.

Storm the beach head of normalcy and find a way to fit back in to his old life again.

He breathed in deeply through his nose and let the doubt creep out between his lips.

Fire Station 23 had been his destination every workday for almost a decade, before he'd had enough of the wanting and not having—before not even having the right to think about Meghan Taylor had dulled his senses so much that he'd been close to becoming a hazard to himself and his team.

And he'd loved being a firefighter. At six-five and a good 250 pounds, he'd always been a physical being. He'd played sports in school, had relished the discipline of the ROTC program that had paid for his degree at KU. He'd opted to join the Corps after graduation, had served in both infantry and artillery support units. When his stint was up and he'd transferred to the Reserves, firefighting had offered the perfect schedule to give him the time off he needed to attend weekend trainings and summer deployments. His engineering degree had taught him how buildings were put together, and how fire and heat, chemicals and explosions could bring them down.

Being a firefighter wasn't all that different from serving his country. He liked using his hands to maintain, deploy and neutralize powerful equipment and dangerous explosives. He thrived on the teamwork involved in attacking the flames, developing close relationships with the men and women he worked with. He loved cooking for his buddies at the firehouse, keeping physically and mentally fit, wearing his uniform proudly, and protecting his city.

Each time the alarm had gone off, he'd eagerly answered the call.

When his country had asked him to go overseas for a year, he'd answered that call, too.

Getting the investigative assignment at Station 23 should feel like a well-earned reward, like he was finally coming home.

John turned off the engine and braced his forearms on the steering wheel to stare through the windshield. In the two years he'd been gone, the city had repainted the firehouse facade a cool steel-gray. He missed the warm, earthy brown of the old bricks. He missed knowing what was going on in the lives of his coworkers, several of whom were now moving in and out of the open bays, washing down one of the engines and trimming up the landscaping in front of the building. He missed knowing exactly what job he was doing and feeling confident that he was the best man for that job. He missed his damn leg and the friends he'd lost in that roadside bombing.

Muttering a curse, John leaned back, dropping his hand to rub his thigh and run his fingers across the elastic band

and molded polymers that added the illusion of a real limb beneath the material of his KCFD-issue cargo pants. He wouldn't be fighting fires anymore with the hardware he was wearing. He'd been *promoted* to arson investigator, a dubious honor that meant KCFD would honor his service to them and to his country, but that there really was no place for him on the front lines of a ladder truck unit anymore.

"You'd best get to it," he chided the hazel eyes squinting back at him in the rearview mirror.

He pulled the brim of his KCFD ball cap low over his forehead and opened the truck door. Despite the handicapped tag stuffed in his glove compartment, John had parked several spaces away from the entrance, giving him time to adjust his stance over his false leg and minimize his limp before approaching the station's open garage doors. The early-evening sky swirled with clouds that hinted at spring showers by nightfall. If he'd been a superstitious man, he'd have seen the coming storm as a bad omen. But John believed in what he could see and touch and trust. He knew this day wasn't going to get any better. The sooner he got this bittersweet reunion with his old job and friends started, the sooner it would end.

"John." As soon as he rounded the corner in front of the fire station, Meghan Wright Taylor set aside the flowers she'd been transferring to a decorative planter and pushed to her feet. Her smile was as sunny as her wavy blond hair as she shucked her gardening gloves and hurried across the driveway to greet him. "I thought my shift was going to end before you got here today." She stretched up on tiptoe to wind her arms around his neck. "It's good to see you."

Although he leaned over to complete the hug, John braced himself to absorb the contact with her shorter frame. Meghan had proved to be a good friend since they'd first been assigned to Ladder Truck 23 together more than fifteen years ago. But her heart had always belonged to one guy, and Gideon Taylor was a smart man to love her just as hard and deep in return.

Even in her black duty uniform, Meghan smelled like the outdoors and sunshine. John released her and stepped away before too many memories and what-ifs got stuck in his head and his first day back at the station turned maudlin. "I like what you've done with the place," he joked.

Meghan laughed and he noted lines of humor beside her warm brown eyes that hadn't been there before. Marriage and motherhood and—cripes, were those captain's bars pinned to her collar?—suited her well.

John flicked his finger beneath her collar, indicating the brass pin she wore. "Somebody got promoted while I was gone."

"This is my station now." She was a smart firefighter, and had earned the respect of her male colleagues long ago. "I'm running the show."

"Congratulations."

"Big John Murdock, I heard you were coming back." John turned at the voice of another familiar friend. Dean Murphy strode out of the garage with a big grin set on his face. "So how are you?"

"Still don't like to be called Big John." Images of tall tales and television commercials had never fit, even when he'd been 100 percent. He clasped hands with the younger man and exchanged a firm handshake. "You still causing trouble around here, Dean?"

Dean had been little more than a rookie before John was deployed. There was a new cloak of maturity around his trim, wiry frame now. "Not much."

"Not much?"

Meghan linked her arm through John's elbow and

pulled him into the station house. "Dean is as much of a player as ever. Claims he wants to settle down and get married before he turns thirty, but I've yet to meet any Mrs. Murphy-to-be."

"You cut me deep, boss." He clasped his hands over his heart in a mock show of pain. "I could settle down if I had to."

"If you had to?" Meghan teased.

Dean winked. "Can I help it if the ladies find me irresistible? I'm just doing my duty to keep 'em all happy."

"As long as you keep doing your job the way you do when you show up at my station house, I don't care how you charm the ladies on your own time." A drumroll of thunder rumbled in the distance and Meghan glanced skyward. "Dean, let's get these trucks back in the house before the rain hits." Her order, gentle yet succinct, got Murphy and some other men moving. But she tugged at John's arm, pulling him away from the sudden bustle of activity around the shiny yellow engines. "Come on, I'll show you your office."

John nodded hellos to old friends and introduced himself to the new hires before following Meghan into the hallway that led to the station offices. A lot had changed on the inside of Station 23 since he'd gone overseas, too. New paint, new staff. Going into an office where he'd work banker's hours and then go home instead of heading for the bunk rooms and lounge areas where the firefighters on seventy-two-hour shift work would sleep and hang out like a family until a call came in.

"We'll get your name and title painted on the door," Meghan promised. He didn't mask his sigh of regret as well as he'd thought. "Does it meet with your approval?"

He must have a thing for freckles on women. The little specks dotting the skin on Meghan's cheeks had been one of the first things he'd noticed about Maggie Wheeler, too. For a brief moment, his head filled with the memory of green eyes, deep and pure in color, wide and frightened and looking to him for answers he couldn't give. But the similarities between his next-door neighbor and the firefighter whose happiness with another man had prompted John to re-up with the Corps ended there. Meghan was sleek and compact while Maggie was tall and rounded. One was a sunny blonde, the other a fiery redhead. One was going out of her way to make him feel welcome while the other...

Hell, he'd never had another woman intrude on his thoughts before when he was with Meghan. The war must have changed him in more ways than he'd realized. Even his ability to concentrate was missing in action. Taken aback by the observation, John covered his surprise by pulling off his KCFD cap and making a joke. "I've been sleeping on cots, the ground or a hospital bed for the past year. Don't know if I can handle a plush leather chair and air-conditioning."

"You've earned the promotion, John."

But it would be a different job. He'd go in and analyze a fire scene after the fact, when his leg wouldn't matter. His days of being on the front line, of being the first man into the action were behind him.

Swallowing the bile of that admission, John tossed his cap onto the desk, claiming the functional office space as his own. "Bare bones but sufficient. Most of my job will be about analysis and writing up reports, so this will do just fine."

If Meghan sensed his melancholy over the irony of returning to work without really getting to do the work he'd been trained for, she hid it behind a smile and invited him next door into her office. In a marked contrast to the bare metal shelves and computer in his office, her space was decorated with awards, family pictures and abundant warmth.

He picked up the framed photo of Meghan surrounded by her husband and four adopted sons. "Good grief, all the boys are taller than you now."

She gently caressed the picture when she returned it to her desk. "They're not boys anymore." She pointed to a wedding photograph on the shelf behind her desk. "Our oldest, Alex, is married now—to a lovely young attorney named Audrey."

John knew the older boys had been teenagers when she and Gideon Taylor had adopted them. Still… "You're not old enough to be a mother-in-law."

Meghan laughed. "Audrey makes it easy. I'm only ten years older than she is so we're more friends than in-laws. And Alex is a SWAT cop now. Hard to believe he was in so much trouble when I worked with him as a foster child. And this one—" she picked up another photo of a tall, muscular police officer with an imposing German shepherd seated beside him "—is Pike. He's K-9 patrol with KCPD." She pointed to another photo, with two teenagers dressed in blue-and-gold letter jackets. "Matthew and Mark were little more than toddlers when Gideon and I adopted them. Now they're in high school."

The love for her family was evident in her voice. John breathed in deeply, wishing that could have been him in those pictures, but knowing he never could have made her happy the way Gideon Taylor did. He'd been relegated to big brother status on the day they'd met, and nothing would ever change that. The pain he used to feel might not grip as tightly as it once had, but it was still there. John covered the inevitable awkwardness with a teasing laugh. "And yet, you don't look a day over twenty-nine."

Meghan joined in. "Thanks, but flattery will get you nowhere. I run a tight ship, Murdock. I'll expect you to fall in line, too, now that you'll be based here. I requested you for my station house, you know."

"I suspected as much."

"We always made a great team fighting fires," Meghan explained. "You were solid, dependable. You grounded everybody here, especially me." She leaned over the desk and dropped her voice to a whisper. "Besides, there's not a one of those goons out there who can cook a meal the way you can. Not even me. And I've had such a hankering for your pork roast with that cheesy polenta and glazed carrots."

Okay, he could do this. He could make nice and be friends and pretend his world hadn't changed. "I'll be sure to check the pantry before the end of the day, boss."

"My taste buds are happier already." She headed out the door. "Come on, I'll show you the new upgrades in the kitchen—"

Forced or friendly conversation of any kind ended abruptly when the station alarm went off. Meghan checked in with the dispatcher and told him to make the call for the full team to suit up and respond to a warehouse fire near the Missouri River. The instinct to run out to the gear lockers in the garage with everyone else jolted through John's legs.

He was following Dean to the first truck when the adrenaline haze cleared and John reminded himself that he was only feeling that jolt in one of his legs. Any *instinct* he felt was all in his imagination. He wasn't cleared for front-line duty. Ever again. The call wasn't his to respond to.

He drifted back out of the way as the men and women climbed into the trucks and paramedic van. The flashing orange lights blurred, and the strident repetition of the alarm muffled his hearing as he faded back into the space vacated by the ambulance.

He startled when Meghan dashed up and touched his arm. "I'll call you myself once the blaze is contained so you can investigate the cause. Depending on the size of the fire, the structural damage and this weather—" she nodded toward the drizzle of rain outside the open garage doors that was coming faster and heavier by the second "—it may be morning before I can safely get you in there."

John nodded and she stepped up onto the running board of the engine and opened the passenger-side door. He limped over to catch the door while she climbed inside. So maybe he had been relegated to chief cook and side-line watcher—he wasn't going to let his punky mood hold anyone up and endanger the lives and property of the people who'd called in the fire.

"Are you all right?" she asked, pulling her hair up into a ponytail inside her white scene commander's helmet.

John closed the door and tapped it twice, giving the driver the all-clear to go. "Go do your job," he urged, then stepped aside. "Watch the roads. They'll be slick with this new rain."

With a nod, she picked up the radio and gave the order, "Let's move out."

The station lights stopped flashing and the alarm went silent as the last of the trucks pulled out, leaving him standing alone in the middle of the empty garage. The sudden silence and frustrated yearning for the life he'd once led filled him up and spilled out into the emptiness surrounding him.

Yeah, this reintegration into civilian life was going real damn well. He was making friends and doing important, useful things with his time.

Sarcasm was eating a hole in his stomach when John heard a telephone ring. He knew there had to be a skeleton crew on hand at the station 24/7. The dispatcher, at least, should still be in his office.

But the phone rang and rang, and no one was answering. Some of that same urgency he'd felt when the alarm had gone off sparked through him again, and he hurried back to the offices to discover that it was the phone on his new desk that was ringing.

No way had Meghan and Company 23 reached the fire, much less put it out. And he didn't know another soul who'd be calling.

The only way to stop the speculation was to pick it up. "Hello?"

"Captain Murdock?"

He'd have written off the young voice as a wrong number or a prank if they hadn't called him by name. "This is John Murdock. Who's asking?"

"Travis Wheeler." Son of a gun. Sergeant Green Eyes' kid was calling him? Why? "I'm your new neighbor, remember?"

"I know who you are, Travis. How did you get this number?"

"You said you worked at Station 23."

Resourceful kid. Admirable stick-to-it-tiveness. Although he wasn't sure if tracking him down through the KCFD help desk or through some online information system irked him or concerned him. John checked his watch. It was after six o'clock. "Are you reporting a fire?"

There was a long pause and a rustling of movement over the phone, as though the kid was moving around. "No, I'm at the ballpark. Abbott Field."

What the heck was going on? "Trav, I'm at work. I can't talk baseball right now."

"It's raining." Probably all across the city by now. "I tried calling my mom, but she didn't answer. Sometimes she has to turn off her cell phone at work, like when she's in a meeting. She didn't answer at home either. It said something was out of service. It didn't even ring."

So he'd managed to get a call through to John at the fire station, but couldn't get a line to his own mother? A vague sense of unease raised the fine hairs at the back of John's neck. First the elevator in their building was out of commission, and now the landline phone wasn't working? Travis had mentioned something on the elevator last week about needing to know a *safe place* where he could go. Those fine hairs jumped to full attention. What the hell was going on next door with Maggie Wheeler? "Why are you looking for your mom? Are you okay? Is *she* okay?"

"I don't know. Practice got done early because of the rain and there's no one here. Well, nobody I know. There are some people who were watching practice still here, but... She was supposed to pick me up, but she's late." Suspecting Travis was standing out in the rain was worrisome enough, but there was something ominous about the pause in the boy's voice. "Mom's never late."

John plucked his hat from the desk and pulled out his keys. "I'm on my way."

Chapter Five

"Are you kidding me? Two cops called my work this afternoon."

Maggie deleted the vile message on her phone and hurried up the steps of the Fourth Precinct parking garage. The clock on her cell phone flipped over to 6:30 as another message from Danny Wheeler began to play. Her uniform and skin were damp from the rain outside, and she could feel the loose hairs sticking to her face kinking into curls. But she hadn't bothered with a jacket or umbrella because she was running so far behind.

"They talked to my parole officer." Danny's voice was full of accusation. "They came to my job. What did you tell them about me, Mags?"

Nothing that wasn't already in his arrest or prison record. But, like usual, if things had gone wrong with Danny's day, it was somehow her fault. And if she hadn't caused the problem, then he expected her to save him from it.

Reaching the third level, she jogged across the concrete toward her truck. She hit Delete again, praying the next message would be another from Travis, telling her that the parents of one of his teammates had agreed to wait with him after all, or had given him a ride home.

If she hadn't been so busy pulling files and going

over them with the detectives, absorbing every nugget of wisdom about what made one convicted rapist a viable suspect and another one not, she would have gotten Travis's call. She would have excused herself from the debriefing with Montgomery and Fensom, even appealed to Chief Taylor if necessary, in order to leave early to pick up her son.

With no update from Travis after his first call, and his cell phone now going straight to voice mail, Maggie quickened her pace. It had always been her and Travis. As his only legal parent, he relied on her entirely for his transportation, food, love and safety. Letting him down, even when the weather and a chain of events beyond her control messed up her schedule, wasn't an option she could live with.

She pulled her keys from her leather shoulder bag and punched the remote to unlock her truck.

Oh, hell. Danny had left yet another message. Whether he was upset about KCPD approaching him over making contact with her or if this was about his being a person of interest in the Rose Red Rapist case didn't matter right now. "...asking me about *my* wife? *My* whereabouts? I remembered your favorite flower, didn't I? You're supposed to have my back, Mags. I am not going back to prison. Understand that? You will not send me back there."

"Officer Wheeler?" Startled by the real voice behind her, Maggie silenced her phone and whirled around. "Maggie Wheeler?"

"Yes?" Settling back into her skin, she made a quick assessment of the man approaching her. His dark hair and easy stride were familiar, although she couldn't place him. Civilian clothes. Unarmed. He looked friendly enough, but something about the piercing blue eyes put her guard up.

"Gabriel Knight. *Kansas City Journal.*" He flashed the

press card hanging alongside a camera around his neck "I've managed to get a few words from the other members of Chief Taylor's task force this week, but you about got away from me."

"I'm off duty now, Mr. Knight." She opened her truck door and dismissed him. "And I need to get going."

"Is everything all right?" He nodded toward the cell phone squeezed in her fist. "You seem upset."

She tucked the phone into her bag and tossed it onto the passenger seat. "I'm fine."

"Just two minutes of your time, Mrs.? Miss—"

"It's *Sergeant* Wheeler." She climbed in behind the wheel. Travis needed her. "And I'm sorry, but I don't have two minutes right now."

When she turned to start the engine, he caught her door and held it open. "Do you think KCPD will have any better luck this time catching the Rose Red Rapist?"

"I hope so. Excuse me." She tugged at the door handle, but the reporter didn't budge.

"You hope so? That doesn't inspire me with confidence, Sergeant Wheeler."

"Well, of course, we're doing everything we can. KCPD's best are on this case, I promise you." She tamped down on the red-haired temper sparking in her blood. No meant no in any situation. What didn't Danny and this guy understand about that? But the first thing she'd learned when she went to work as a KCPD desk sergeant was that she was the face of KCPD most people saw. And that meant she had to be a friendly, helpful, patient face. So she drummed up a smile for the reporter. "Do you mind?"

"If this is an example of the department's best work, then what is someone with virtually no investigative experience like you doing on the task force?" Maggie's fingers tightened around the steering wheel at the low blow to the department and to her. "Is it because your ex-husband served time for rape? Is he a suspect?"

There went *friendly*. "Mr. Knight—"

"I hear you have a real knack for getting the victims of these crimes, like Bailey Austin, to open up and answer questions. Can you tell me why that is? Why did you get results when a dozen other cops before you couldn't?"

"How do you know about—?"

"So you did interview Bailey Austin."

Helpful was off the table now, too. "There are confidentiality expectations in place with assault victims, Mr. Knight. Now remove your hand from my door before I arrest you."

He let go of the door but didn't move to give her enough room to close it. "Threatening the press? That ought to make a good headline."

And now *patience* was done. "Headline this—Single Mom Needs to Pick Up Son from Ball Practice. I have to go. You should speak to Dr. Kate Kilpatrick." She pointed toward the precinct headquarters building across the street. "She's the task force's liaison with the press. She can answer your questions better than I can."

He finally retreated. "You've given me more than enough to work with, Sergeant Wheeler. Have a pleasant evening."

Maggie's response wasn't nearly so civil. She slammed the door and peeled out of the parking garage, leaving Gabriel Knight and whatever he was texting on his phone behind her.

She hadn't expected to be interviewed by a reporter and hadn't handled it well at all. He'd gotten her while she was distracted with Travis and Danny, and had ferreted out answers she wasn't sure she was supposed to give. All her thoughts were exploding in a swirling mass of temper, frustration, self-doubts and second-guessing. She hated feeling out of control like this. She was a good mother. A good cop. She'd make a good detective, too.

But knowing the truth and feeling the truth were two different things. And right now, it was impossible to silence the taunts from the corners of her mind. Taunts that echoed in Danny's derisive voice.

Your child is stranded in the rain.

You just botched that press interview.

You will never get anything right on your own.

"Shut up, Danny." Voice in her head or face-to-face terror, he wasn't going to undermine her confidence anymore.

Maggie turned on her headlights and cranked the windshield wipers to give her a clearer view through the rainy streets that led to the ballpark near Travis's school. As the snail's pace of rush-hour traffic stopped her at yet another light, she toyed with the idea of sticking the magnetized flashers on her roof and turning on the siren. Instead of abusing her badge and busting through the line of cars, she picked up her purse.

Concentrating on evening out her breathing and keeping her panic in check, she pulled out her phone and continued checking her messages. There were three more from Danny, probably as sweetly apologetic as the first three had been rife with anger and accusation. She deleted all the messages once she saw that there were no more from her son.

Easing along with the flow of traffic, she called Travis's number again, forcing herself to keep thinking positive thoughts when it went straight to voice mail. Had he let the battery run down? Forgotten to turn it on? Had he set it down someplace and lost it, leaving him not only abandoned but also unable to contact her? She left a message just in case. "I'm so sorry I'm running behind, sweetie, but I'm on my way. Make sure you stay where the lights are and hang out with your friends if they're still there. I love you."

She called the apartment again to see if he'd found a way home but got a recorded message about the line being out of order. A follow-up call to Joe Standage gave her an answering machine message. She left a request asking him to check why her home phone wasn't working, and if he saw Travis at the apartment, to please call her. She was praying for a cut utility line or an incompetent building super, and not something more sinister.

But she'd once had a daughter, too. And even though Danny hadn't killed little Angel himself, he hadn't been above using his own daughter as leverage to ensure Maggie's cooperation. Danny said he wanted to meet, and she'd said no. If he'd taken Travis to punish or persuade her…

Maggie cursed rush hour and pressed a little harder on the accelerator.

Once she crossed over the I-70 overpass and veered off toward the east side of the city, traffic thinned. A glimpse of white in her rearview mirror made her vaguely aware of a square van a few vehicles back making the same turns she was. But there was still some going-home traffic in the area, and several cars were heading northeast like she was, so she dismissed it.

She was on her third unanswered call to her son when she turned into the parking lot at Abbott Field and saw that the ball field lights were off. The concrete concession stand and batting cages were dark and locked up tight, and the bleachers and dugouts were all deserted. With the clouds blocking off the last dregs of daylight, the only illumination came from the distant streetlamps and her truck's headlights. "Where are you, Travis?" she muttered in hushed fear before finally thinking clearly enough to dial a different number. "Coach Hernandez?"

Laughter in the background nearly drowned out his reply. "Mrs. Wheeler. Did you rethink dinner?"

Right. He'd taken his son to a Scout meeting. "Is Travis with you?"

"What? We're going to that pizza place over on Independence Avenue."

"I'm not interested in dinner, Coach." She tried not to scream her own frustration. "Is Travis there?"

"No."

"Then where is he? I came as soon as I got his message about practice ending early. I can't believe you'd let a little boy stay at the ballpark alone."

"I thought you'd already picked him up." His tone bristled at her criticism, and he was quick to defend himself. "Everyone was gone when I left."

"Gone?" Oh, Lord. She willed herself X-ray vision as she peered through the windshield and the rain. "*I'm* at the park right now and no one's here. Do you know who he got a ride home with?"

"No." Travis's coach must have walked out of the meeting because the background suddenly quieted. "I saw him making a phone call. I just assumed it was to you."

How could the man *just assume* her child was safe? But the priority was finding Travis right now, not arguing Michael Hernandez's fitness to be a coach responsible for her child's well-being. "All right. Thank you."

"Mrs. Wheeler?"

"I have to go."

"Let me know when you find—"

She disconnected the call and tried to think like a cop instead of a terrified mother. With her heart pounding in time to the quick rhythm of the windshield wipers, she pulled her KCPD windbreaker from behind the seat and grabbed a flashlight from the glove compartment. She left the headlights on but locked the doors when she climbed out to begin her search of the grounds.

The rain cooled her skin but did nothing to ease her anxiety. With her emotions so out of focus, she relied on her training to do a quick, methodical search of the park. The doors to the main facility were locked, the stands empty. She checked behind trees and trash cans and walked through both the men's and women's public restrooms. The ladder up to the scoreboard was empty. There was no glove, no bat, no balls, no backpack—no sign of a ten-year-old boy anywhere.

"Travis, where are you?"

With the rain washing away the traces of anyone having been at the ball field at all, Maggie headed back to the parking lot and her truck. Maybe she should call in for police assistance. Or go straight to the dispatch office and issue an Amber Alert. Maybe she should get on the phone and call every friend of Travis, every teacher, every human being her son knew to find out if anyone had seen him.

Or maybe, possibly…she should call Danny. He'd never been interested in having children. Angel had been an unfortunate accident in his book. And Travis wasn't even legally his. But Travis knew the name of the man who'd fathered him and knew he was now out on parole. Tension bubbled in her stomach at the idea of the two of them even meeting, much less calling on an absent, worthless father for help.

That's when she saw the white van. Again. *Boyle's Extermination Company,* with the logo of a bug and a rat painted on the side. It was parked out on the street, not half a block away from her truck. Too close to be a coincidence. Someone *had* been following her.

Going on alert when the van's front door slid open, Maggie lifted the hem of her jacket and unsnapped the cover on her holster. She made sure she had access to the radio clipped to her shoulder and shined the beam of her flashlight straight into the face of the stocky man who climbed out.

The light reflected off big, round eyes, vaguely reminiscent of one of the critters on the side of the van. Dressed in tan coveralls, the man hunched his shoulders against the rain and called to her across the parking lot. "Mrs. Wheeler?"

Conquering the urge to retreat at hearing her name on the stranger's lips, she braced her legs and straightened to her full height. The exterminator, according to the matching vermin logo on his coveralls, wasn't any taller than she was, but he was built like an ox. The bug eyes and the tattoos on the side of his neck warred with his friendly smile and the bouquet of roses in his left hand.

Van? Roses? Woman alone?

Maggie put up her hand to stop him from coming any closer. "Do I know you?"

"Lawrence Boyle. I'm a friend of your husband."

"I don't have a husband."

He laughed. "Danny said you'd say that. Here." He held out the drooping red blooms.

"I hate flowers."

When she made no move to take the gift, he laid them across the corner of her truck and tailgate, then shoved his hands into his pockets and backed up a couple of steps.

She wrapped her fingers around the butt of her gun and unsheathed it a few inches. "Keep your hands where I can see them, please."

The bug eyes darted to her weapon. "I'm trying to do you a favor, Mrs. Wheeler. I know we've never met, but I feel like I know you. I know things weren't always great between you and Danny."

"Hands, Mr. Boyle."

"He talks about you all the time." The exterminator with the bleached-white hair pulled his hands from his pockets, then leisurely laced his fingers together and rested them on top of his head.

He'd done that for a police officer before, Maggie noted, keeping him in her sights and inching to the back of the truck. The rain shredded the tissue paper as she pulled it aside to retrieve the note. The *Sorry. Love you* wasn't as troubling as recognizing the card from a florist shop in her neighborhood and knowing Danny had been within a block of her apartment. Had Danny made contact with Travis? Had he done something to keep her from reaching her son?

"He says he's sorry if he said or did anything that upset you today." Lawrence Boyle's hands went right back to the top of his head when she swung the flashlight back to his face. "I guess cops and lawyers make him nervous. He hopes the two of you could have a conversation sometime."

"Not likely." It wasn't the first time Danny had sent flowers as an apology for his unspeakable behavior, but she intended it to be the last. She eyed the van behind Boyle and wondered if her ex was in there, watching her right now. "Where is he?"

"At work by now, I imagine. I gave him a job a few weeks ago. Danny and I go way back."

Judging by the twining blue-and-green tats on his neck, including a trio of teardrops that indicated years of incarceration, she could imagine where they'd met. Just how much did he and Danny have in common? Did they share a penchant for hurting women? "I need you to step back inside your van, Mr. Boyle."

Although he wiped the moisture from his face and re-treated a step, the conversation wasn't over. "Your kid has a strong arm. Can't hit worth crap, though."

Don't ask. The answer will only upset you. "How do you know that?"

"We watched practice for a while. Before the rain started."

We? As in Boyle *and* Danny?

The rain soaking through her uniform was suddenly cold against her skin. "Did Danny take Travis?"

"No, ma'am. I sent him back to the shop to clean up for the day, and cool off."

"Why were you following me?"

"To give you the flowers." He made a face as if that had been a stupid question. "I was taking them to the police station to deliver 'em when I saw you leave. Please, ma'am, they're getting ruined."

Think, Maggie. Think. She had to push through the haze of fear, anger and suspicion to find her son. Did she take his word about Danny's whereabouts or insist on checking the inside of his van?

When he moved toward the flowers again, she pulled her gun and he stopped. His hands went up in the air. "Easy there, Mrs. Wheeler. I don't mean you no harm. You're just worried about your boy, I bet. Danny said you were doing a good job with the kid."

Ultimately, a dubious witness was better than no witness at all. She had to ask, "Did you see my son leave the ballpark?"

"Yeah." Lawrence Boyle lowered his hands and slipped them into the pockets of his coveralls, despite her warning. "Some cripple in a black truck picked him up. Big guy—looked pissed off. Walking on a stick for a leg would put me in a mood, too."

Relief warred with anger inside her. *Cripple?* Lawrence Boyle could only be talking about one man. John Murdock. "That big guy is a war hero. And here's what Danny can do with his flowers."

She knocked the bouquet into a puddle beside her truck, climbed inside and drove away

"TRAVIS RYNE WHEELER, you couldn't have called me half an hour ago to let me know you were safe?" Maggie snapped into her phone. She was immediately contrite over raising her voice, but her emotions were still bubbling too close to the surface. Knowing that Danny had been at the park watching her son, and could have easily been the one offering him a ride home, had terrified her. She should be grateful Travis had had the sense to call someone more reliable. "Sweetie, do you know how crazy I've been with worry?"

"That's why John made me call you." His man-sized sigh made her wonder if there was a big, unsmiling marine standing over him as he spoke. "I left my phone out in the rain and I couldn't see the screen, and did you know none of the phones on the seventh floor are working? John asked Miss Applebaum and the Wongs, too."

"Nice try, pal. But you and I are going to have a refresher course in where and how you can reach me, no matter what you do to your cell phone or what happens in this old building." She reached the sixth-floor landing and paused to control her breathing after her evening sprint. "And we're going to talk about who's a stranger and who you can trust."

"Mom, I know that stuff. That's why I called John. Firefighter? Captain? Duh."

"Then you need a reminder about who you shouldn't be imposing on. Honey, we barely know him." Despite the burn in her thigh muscles, she stretched her legs to take the last flight of stairs two at a time. Time to end the call. "I'm here. You stay put."

Maggie shoved open the door and plowed into the super, Joe Standage. Her cell phone flew across the carpeted floor, a tray of tools spilled in a noisy avalanche and a stepladder crashed into the opposite wall.

"Sorry. Are you all right?"

"Where's the fire?" he asked, pushing himself upright.

Maggie was quicker to get back to her feet. She scooped up pliers and a screwdriver and dropped them into the tray, then slid her hand beneath Mr. Standage's wiry arm to help him up. The peppering of gray in his ruffled hair was a closer match to the arthritic knees that made him slow to stand. But the surprising fitness of his arm muscles made her think his turtle-paced, aw-shucks demeanor was more about personality than age. "Long day. I wasn't looking," she apologized. "Are you okay?"

"I'm fine. Been doing some work for Miss Applebaum in 716. She fried up another batch of those apple fritters." He straightened his clothes and picked up his tool tray. "I put in a call to the phone company to have those phones up and running again by morning. I must have accidentally severed a line when I was cutting through a wall to move the cable for her. Got the elevator fixed, though. Found a disconnected wire. No need for you to be taking the stairs anymore, Mrs. Wheeler. Say, have you had any trouble with ants? Miss Applebaum pulled out the sugar when she was baking and found a whole trail—"

While Joe chatted away, Maggie handed him the folded stepladder. The retired gentleman might have time for a friendly confab, but she didn't. Besides, after that weird encounter with Lawrence Boyle, bugs were the last thing she wanted to think about right now.

"My apologies again." Maggie scooped up her cell phone and hurried past her own apartment door.

"Don't you want to know about the ants?"

Ignoring the older man, Maggie knocked on the door of Apartment 709. "Travis?" She pushed her damp hair off her face and knocked again. "Travis, are you in there?"

Miss Applebaum opened the door behind Maggie and poked her wrinkled nose beneath the security chain. "Is everything all right, dear? I heard a crash. It's not that elevator again, is it?"

"No, ma'am. Joe says it's working now. Travis?" Maggie knocked again. If her son had added a lie about his whereabouts on top of everything else that had happened this evening…

"Now what?" a new voice asked. "Are the phones working yet?"

Miss Applebaum raised her tinny voice. "No, Bernard. Joe had to call the phone company for assistance."

Heat crept into Maggie's cheeks as two more doors in the hallway opened. "Come on, sweetie. Travis?"

The door of 709 suddenly opened in front of her raised fist and she punched John Murdock in the middle of the chest. The big man filled the doorway. He wore a barbecue apron beneath the belt of his jeans and was drying his hands on a towel.

Maggie pulled her hand back. "I'm sorry. Is Trav—"

"He's here. He's safe."

The concise words had no time to register before his hazel eyes darted to the left and the right. Instinctively, Maggie turned her gaze to follow his lead. Miss Applebaum was still checking on the commotion in the hallway. Bernard Cutlass stood in his pajamas and groused about rude people and needing to call his daughter in Belton. Joe Standage was holding the elevator doors open; his face was wreathed with concern. One by one she became aware of eyes at each of the occupied apartments on the seventh floor.

"It's just a miscommunication, folks." John's big hand closed around Maggie's wrist, the warmth and sureness of his touch jolting her again. "Everything's all right."

He pulled her inside and shut the door behind her before letting go. He angled his head down to hers, filling up her vision with a square jaw and narrowed eyes. "Did I just lie to those people? Or does every evening here have this much drama?"

"I'm sorry I hit you. Where's my son?"

The square jaw backed away. "Kitchen."

Maggie darted through the apartment, its layout mirroring hers next door, and found Travis at the table, doing his homework. "Hi, Mom."

"*Hi, Mom?* That's all you have to say?" Clothes were dry, face was smiling. He looked normal and safe and content, and she wrapped her arms around him and hugged him.

"Told you she'd be worried." John moved past them to check something on the stove. Maggie pulled Travis to his feet, nestled her cheek against his thick, damp hair and hugged him even tighter. "As soon as I realized you didn't know he'd called me, I had him use my cell phone."

"Do you have any idea how scared I was?"

Sooner than she wanted, Travis wriggled free. "Mom, jeez."

Maggie captured his chin in the palm of her hand and looked down into his sweet green eyes. "Don't you ever do anything like that again. I went to the ballpark. I couldn't find you. You wouldn't answer your phone."

"I couldn't." He squinched his face up in apology and sat back at the table.

"Coach Hernandez should never have left you…" *Cool it, Maggie.* The coach was someone Travis looked up to. She shoved aside the tendrils of hair sticking to her damp skin. "It was getting dark and it was raining and there was a man there—"

"What man?" Casual though an apron and soup ladle might make him appear, there was a probing intensity in John's eyes that reached her clear across the room. "The last couple of vehicles were leaving when I picked him up. No one was in the stands."

Maggie shivered at the assessing gaze that pierced through the armor she wore, inside and out. But she shook her head, dismissing his concern. Danny Wheeler and Lawrence Boyle and lousy timing were her problems, not his. She wound her arms around her own waist, trying to alleviate a chill that couldn't be entirely blamed on the wet clothes she wore.

"You're all I have, sweetie. And with work and that reporter and…" She fisted her hands beneath her crossed arms so she wouldn't embarrass Travis with another hug. "I couldn't find you. I didn't know you were safe."

"I borrowed Juan's phone to call the fire station and John came and got me. I took care of the situation myself. You don't have to worry about me." He did a very good imitation of mature, but his next sentence reassured her that Travis was still her little boy. "And please don't call me sweetie." His eyes flicked to the man at the stove and he dropped his voice to a whisper. "Not in front of other people."

A relieved laugh sneaked out. She just couldn't resist reaching out and mussing his hair with her fingers. She felt the dampness of it and remembered she must look like a waterlogged mess herself. "You're ten years old, not thirty. *I'm* supposed to take care of *you*."

John set down the ladle and joined them at the table. "Come on, slugger. Finish that last problem so I can clear things off and set the table." He looked over the top of Travis's head to Maggie. "You two want to stay for dinner?"

Another dinner invitation from a man? When had she ever been this popular? And when had it ever been a good idea for her to think about saying yes?

"Please, Mom?"

The tug at her sleeve wasn't nearly as persuasive as the warmth that spread through her beneath John Murdock's focused attention. As her fear for her son's safety dissipated, other sensations were sneaking in—like the way John hadn't budged when she'd knocked on his chest. Like the distinctly masculine hills and hollows filling out his khaki-green T-shirt, and the way the color of the cotton intensified the pale green of his acutely observant gaze. And she couldn't help but notice that he was tall enough that even she had to tip her chin to see the color and expression of those intriguing eyes.

That surprising appreciation about a man made her self-conscious about how she must look. The rain had probably washed away what little makeup she did wear. Damp strands of hair had escaped from her bun and kinked around her face and collar. And even though it hadn't mattered for a long time, she knew her mannish uniform, thick belt and Kevlar transformed her figure into something about as feminine as the long plank table between them.

No, she needed to get out of here before she did something silly like accept his invitation. Travis was the only guy she needed in her life.

"We wouldn't want to impose."

"Aw, Mom." Travis moaned on three different pitches.

"I wouldn't have invited you if it was an imposition.

Food's made. There's plenty. Stay and eat. Or don't." John's matter-of-fact offer was an embarrassing reminder that he hadn't asked her on a date. This was about food, practicality and being kind. And they'd have a ten-year-old chaperon, for Pete's sake.

She must be in a pretty vulnerable state to be worrying about such things around a man who was more stranger than friend. Yet he'd rescued her son. He'd answered the call to protect the most precious thing in her life when she hadn't been there to rescue him herself. He'd touched her, and she hadn't minded. He didn't remind her of Danny Wheeler in any way.

Moody as he seemed to be, John Murdock was a good, decent man. Maggie had known far too few of those in her life. Maybe that's all this sudden attraction was. He was a good guy, the kind of man she wanted her son to know. The kind of man who should be their friend.

And whatever he was cooking, it really did smell wonderful. That was some kind of spicy stew, and corn bread if she wasn't mistaken. Her empty stomach grumbled in noisy appreciation. Oh, yeah, she was a real catch right now. Like she should worry about becoming anything more than friends.

"Do you have honey to go with that corn bread?" she asked.

"I bet I could find some packed in a box somewhere."

"Does that mean we can stay?" Travis really did seem to like the guy, and John didn't seem to mind the adulation.

"Can you give me five minutes to change into some dry clothes?"

John nodded.

"All right, then. We'll stay."

"Yes!"

Maggie rested a hand on Travis's shoulder to calm him down. "Just for dinner. We don't want to take up any more of John's time. And you and I will clean up the kitchen afterward."

Travis's groan was as loud as his cheer had been.

John grinned, transforming his chiseled features into something quite handsome and making her pulse trip over itself when he turned that smile on her. "Sounds like a deal to me."

"Finish your homework." She sat Travis back in his chair and returned to the living room. John followed her out to escort her to the door.

She'd been in such a rush on the way in that she hadn't paid any attention to the decor. While she had to admire a man who could move in one day and have most of his stuff unpacked and put away so quickly, she wondered at the lack of personal touches. The only shots of color in the room were the spines on a collection of books that filled an entire shelf from floor to ceiling—and the rich navy blue of his Marine Corps uniform in a plastic cleaner's bag draped over the back of the couch.

"That's impressive." Drawn to the subtle display of pride and patriotism, she detoured to the sofa to get a closer look at the brass buttons and royal blue slacks with the red stripe down the side.

"Just got them out of storage yesterday."

"My dad was a marine, too. But his uniform was a little different—he was enlisted."

"Ooh-rah." John stopped at the front door and turned. "Where did he serve?"

"Quartermaster Corps out in Barstow." She blinked away the grim memories of her teen years in Southern California. "He was killed in a motorcycle accident off base."

"I'm sorry."

Soon after, she'd met a young Navy seaman named Danny Wheeler, who'd seemed like the answer to her heartbreak. Her late mother had approved of Danny, had told her it would be good to have a man in the family again. Thank God her mother hadn't lived to see how her marriage to Danny had turned out.

Maggie blinked again and forced herself to concentrate on the computer-generated pattern of grays and tans on John's utility work uniform. She gently shifted the carefully pressed dress blues aside to get a better look. "Even the camouflage looks different from what Dad wore. That was a different generation, I guess."

Beneath the camo uniform she found an open box. She immediately recognized the Purple Heart container and reached inside to retrieve it. Danny had burned her father's service mementos one drunken night in an effort to keep her from putting any other man before him. She blinked away that raw memory, too. "Dad had one of these from his tour of duty in Vietnam. Before I was born."

She couldn't help but let her gaze slide over to the denim pant leg that folded in around John's artificial limb. "Can I ask what happened? Does it still hurt?"

John crossed the living room and plucked the felt box from her fingers. "That's a conversation for another night."

She noticed the felt covers of several other medals when he placed the Purple Heart back inside the moving box.

"Are you pinning these on your uniform?"

"No. Just haven't got them put away yet."

Another medal case caught her eye and she reached inside to pick it up. Her neighbor was even more of a hero than she'd defended against Lawrence Boyle that evening. "But you should, Captain. At least put them in a display cabinet. A Silver Star is something to be proud—"

He grabbed the medal and dumped it back with the others. Then he quickly scooped up the box and uniforms, shoved them in the front closet and shut the door—taking away any trace that he was a military man...beyond the buzz cut of pecan-brown hair and the proud carriage of those broad shoulders. "It's just John, remember? You'd better get out of those wet things before dinner gets cold."

"I'm sorry if I said something wrong. I was just admiring—"

"You didn't say anything wrong." He drilled her with a look that told her his words weren't entirely true.

She'd touched a nerve. But as someone who'd completely fried her own nerves for the day, she understood his need to avoid touchy subjects right now. She headed for the door he held open for her. "Okay, Just John. Thank you—for everything this evening. I'm not used to depending on anyone else." She wanted to say or do more, but the steely cast to those suddenly cold eyes told her that no apology would be welcome. So she opted for a simple smile and a quick exit. "I'll be back in a few minutes."

Chapter Six

11:47 p.m. John read the time on the table beside his bed and tried to remember the last time he'd gone this long without checking a clock or watch and wondering when something would end—like lying in a burning vehicle and listening to his comrades dying, pushing himself to the limits during a painful physical-therapy session, or working side by side with Meghan Taylor and pretending he didn't care.

But tonight he hadn't thought about time. He hadn't thought about Meghan. He hadn't really thought much about the war he'd left behind. There'd been no past to grieve or regret, no future to worry about. For a few hours tonight, he'd simply lived in the moment.

Dinner with the Wheelers had been surprisingly relaxing and fun and…distracting. Maggie was true to her word, taking only a few minutes to change and come back. She'd washed away the smudges of mascara that had shadowed the freckles beneath her eyes. And even though she hadn't released her hair from that practical bun she liked to wear, it was nice to see her in civvies and discover that the curvy hips and butt down below were balanced with equally sweet curves on top.

Not that he'd complimented her or flirted. He'd just noticed. A lot. He'd noticed the way she'd loaded up her corn bread with honey, and then licked the sweet golden mess off her fingers. She was genuinely pretty and unpretentious and crazy about her son.

And yeah, maybe his ego had taken a few strokes when he'd caught a soft smile or curious glance directed his way. But he wasn't looking for a relationship or date, or even the chance to exercise some of the other parts of his body that hadn't seen any action since the roadside bomb outside that Afghan village. He didn't need to be with anyone until he was sure his body could keep up with his brain, and he was certain he could keep the demons that sometimes still haunted him back in the past where they belonged.

Besides, Travis Wheeler had demanded the bulk of his attention at the dinner table. The boy had thoroughly tested John's knowledge of all things baseball, and only the promise of spending some time in the batting cage with him before his game on Thursday night had finally been enough to let John turn the dinner conversation to something other than sports.

Not that Maggie let the discussion stray to anything deeper than the jovial incompetence of their building super. Joe Standage was as friendly and helpful as they came, but it had already been a comedy of errors when it came to fixing things around here. The elderly lady whose apartment sat kitty-corner from John's had complained about a leaky toilet and wound up having to replace her entire bathroom floor after a visit from Joe. Then there was the stuck elevator, and the phones that were still out of order. He'd gone down to the basement himself to inspect the leads running through the building. Judging by the sloppy work he'd seen, the super was lucky that his power saw had cut through a telephone line instead of one carrying electricity to the seventh floor. Could the guy in charge of building maintenance really make so many mistakes? Or was someone deliberately sabotaging things on the seventh floor, leaving Joe to clean up afterward?

John had learned several other things about the tenants on the seventh floor. Maggie had warned him to expect gifts of baked good from Miss Applebaum. And that the Wongs would probably not come out of their apartment to interact with him, but that they would somehow know everything that was going on in the building anyway. Bernie Cutlass talked like a grouch, but he'd been a heck of a lot friendlier before his wife of fifty-some years had passed away last year.

John had learned that Travis loved science and math but thought reading was for girls. After the meal, he'd introduced Travis to his library in the living room, earning a hidden thumbs-up from Maggie. Then she'd insisted on putting away the food and loading the dishwasher by herself, urging John to keep her son interested in the books on his shelves. He'd been happy to lend Travis a couple of YA books—one about a dog who was adopted by an Army unit, and a classic fantasy by Madeleine L'Engle.

Inevitably Travis's curiosity about his injuries came up. And while *transtibial amputation* had tongue-tied the boy, pulling up his pant leg to let him inspect the knee joint and composite rod, as well as letting him inspect the specialized blade prosthetic John used when he was running or working out had kept him talking right up until the moment Maggie had to literally pull him out the door with reminders of brushing teeth and bedtime.

John slipped his bookmark between the pages of the novel he was reading and set it aside to ponder what it was about the family next door that could divert his attention even now that all was quiet on the other side of the bedroom wall that separated his apartment from theirs.

Maggie had been relaxed and friendly at dinner, curious

to hear about his sister's upcoming wedding; sympathetic to learn that he'd lost his parents as a teenager, too. She'd liked his cooking and was surprised to learn that he was the self-taught chef of the family who'd honed his gourmet skills by watching television and preparing dinners for his coworkers at the fire station.

John inhaled a deep, settling breath as he recalled the lines of strain beside those striking green eyes and pale rose lips. Most of Maggie Wheeler's relaxed charm had been an act.

He speculated about the weird convergence of events surrounding the lady cop. If there were enough strange things going on to make him suspicious, then she must be downright paranoid.

Something about night patrols and trusting his gut and experience more than he trusted his eyes and ears told him there was trouble lurking at the fringes of Maggie's life. The woman was hiding a secret or two. She'd been terrified that her son had been alone at the ballpark and out of contact with her. She'd mentioned a mysterious man. The woman wore a gun, a badge and body armor, yet she'd just about had a nervous breakdown when that elevator had gotten stuck.

John eyed the stump of his leg beneath the hem of the running shorts he wore to bed. He was hardly the warrior he'd once been, but he had a feeling that woman's troubles were going to nag at him until he had answers. In every cell of his body he'd been trained to rescue and protect. And while life had altered how he could respond, the instincts were still there.

Maybe that's all this bout of insomnia was—his instincts warring with his abilities. He was aware that Maggie had stirred something in him—a fact that was playing hell with his long-held assumption that Meghan

Taylor was the only female who would ever turn his head. And he knew Maggie was in trouble. But even though her son had invited him into their lives, she hadn't asked for his help. Hell, he wasn't even sure what he could do for her beyond volunteering for a little after-school transportation and some male role modeling for Travis.

Would that be enough to satisfy those protective instincts? That need to take action that drummed through his blood? Shouldn't the offer of neighborly friendship be enough to appease those rusty urges before he embarrassed himself by attempting to do things he was no longer capable of?

A telephone rang in the bedroom behind the thin wall, breaking the silence of the night and giving John his answers.

His hands stiffened into fists at his sides as he glanced at the clock. Midnight. They'd been hours without a line to the outside world, and now, at precisely 12:00 a.m. the phone was ringing in Maggie Wheeler's bedroom?

He swung a leg and a half off the side of the bed and reached for a shoe and the prosthetic propped against the bedside table. For months he'd attuned his ears to the subtlest nuances of sound, warning him of enemy movement in the middle of the night. For years before that, he'd learned to pick up on the sounds of human distress amidst the popping and crashing sounds of a burning building and roaring fire hose.

John concentrated on the methodical process of twisting the prosthetic into place until the suction of the tailored fit engaged, locking the false leg to his own.

Don't listen. Don't eavesdrop. Don't notice.

But the ringing phone wasn't half as alarming as the panicked words he couldn't quite make out, followed by a slamming sound and a scramble through drawers and a closet next door.

He couldn't wait and wonder. It wasn't in him to sit and do nothing. Something was wrong. Something was very wrong.

John pulled the elastic band into place over his knee joint, grabbed his T-shirt from the foot of the bed and hurried out the door. A quick glance up and down the hallway revealed no signs of movement, only shadows and the security light by the elevator doors. Was that…

His eyes zeroed in on the door to the stairwell next to the elevator. Had he imagined that gap between the door and frame? A sliver of light from the landing blinking out as the door closed?

"Hey!" His hopping, hobbling gait got him to the end of the hall in a matter of seconds and he pushed open the swinging steel door. The staccato of running feet echoed up from several stories below. What the hell? John jumped down to the third step in pursuit of whoever had been lurking on their floor. He nearly pitched forward on the fourth step, caught himself on the sixth and slowed his pace to keep his balance as he circled the middle landing.

Frustration poured through his system, telling his body to go faster. Maybe if he'd had on his running leg, he might have a chance of catching the guy. But the perp was speeding up and he was slowing down. John was halfway to the fifth floor when he heard a door slam open down below. The distant door closed again and he knew he'd never be able to catch the guy.

Swallowing his pride and changing strategy, John switched course and jogged back up the stairs. There was still no other sign of activity on the seventh floor when he stopped in front of Maggie's door. He knocked softly. Knocked again. "Maggie?"

He heard a shuffle of noise from inside the apartment, including one unmistakable rasp and click of metal on metal. John had been in the military long enough to recognize the sound of a bullet sliding into the chamber of a semiautomatic. He stepped to one side of the door, out of the potential line of fire, and knocked again. "Maggie, it's John. You can lower your weapon. Open up."

A shadow passed over the peephole, then the chain and dead bolt disengaged and the door opened. Wavy copper hair hung loose and danced over the dotted skin of Maggie's shoulder. She wore long pajama pants, a pair of tank tops and carried her GLOCK 9 down at her side. She'd opened the door just wide enough to flash him a smile he didn't buy. "It's late."

He wedged his shoulder against the door to keep her from closing it. "Tell me about it. You went to bed an hour ago."

"How do you know?"

"Old construction and thin walls. Your bedroom butts up to mine."

Her cheeks flooded with heat, and then he felt her shoving against the door. "Well…stop listening in, you Peeping Tom. Or whatever you call a spy like you."

What John lacked in speed and grace he made up for in brute strength. He planted his foot, braced his hand against the doorjamb and refused to retreat. "Look, I'm not the only one spying on—"

Her telephone rang again. She was wound up tight enough for him to see the leap of muscles beneath her skin. Then her shoulders sagged with some sort of surrender and she swung open the door. "Come on in. I don't want to wake Travis."

John closed the door behind him and threw the dead bolt while Maggie dashed into the kitchen to pick up the phone. "Hello?" He reached the archway into the kitchen in time to see her steady her posture and repeat the greeting. "Hello?"

The color draining from her cheeks told him as much as the gun in her hand that these late-night calls weren't a wrong number. Without breaking stride or asking permission, John plucked the phone from her hand and demanded an answer. "Who is this?"

A startled huff followed by the sounds of labored breathing were punctuated by a man's voice. "You can't have her. She's mine or nobody's."

Adrenaline burned through John's veins at the stark threat. "Listen, you son of a—"

The line abruptly disconnected.

John replaced the cordless phone in its charger, making a quick note that the woman needed caller ID before facing her. "Maggie?"

"What did he say?" She was staring at the phone, rubbing her free hand up and down her right arm. She shook as though a cruel prankster had just dropped a bucket of ice down her back.

"Doesn't matter." John reached out to touch her shoulder and she turned and walked right into his chest. Automatically, his arms wound around her. The thin layers of material between them gave him a clear impression of her healthy curves, shower-fresh scent and trembling fear. It was choice, not instinct, that made him shift his stance to draw her more fully against him and rest his chin at the crown of her soft, fragrant hair.

He didn't know what kind of danger this woman was facing, but he'd be damned if she'd face it alone. He felt a sob of heat against his neck, but there were no tears falling. She was rattled, stunned, too cold for his liking.

"Who was that? Same guy who called before?" He

gently pried the gun from her grasp and she curled all ten
fingers into the front of his T-shirt, burrowing against his
neck and chest. Her breath stuttered across his skin like a
whispered caress. Her hips and thighs lined up squarely
against his as if she'd been built to fit his big, brawny
frame, yet there was no doubt that she was feminine and
soft in every way he was not. He set the gun on the counter
and flattened his palm near the small of her back, along
the cool strip of skin exposed beneath the hem of her shirts
and the low waist of her cotton pants. And even though
his body awakened and warmed at the needy, full-body
contact, John wanted answers. "Easy, Sarge. You're okay
now. You tell me who was on the phone, what he said to
you and what the hell is going on around here that has you
so spooked."

"THERE WAS SOMEONE OUTSIDE? Why didn't you say something?"

Maggie picked up her gun from the counter, reloaded
the magazine John had pulled out for safety's sake, and
dashed out of the kitchen. Parts of her were still a little
numb, a little in shock from the midnight phone calls and
how easily she'd turned to John for comfort. And parts of
her were firing with a panicked need to find where these
threats were coming from and squash them into dust.

"You were a little preoccupied." John followed her into
the living room. "He was there a few minutes ago, before
I knocked. That guy is long gone."

She wouldn't believe it unless she saw it with her own
eyes. If Danny had gotten this close to her home, this close
to Travis…

"Why didn't you tell me there was an intruder in the
building? Did you call 9-1-1?" She stopped at the front
closet and slipped into her running shoes and windbreaker.

She grabbed her keys and badge, stuffed them into a pocket and opened the front door.

John's big hand reached around her and caught the door before she could get out. "You're chasing down a perp in your PJs?"

The square jaw and hazel eyes and look that said she was behaving irrationally were right there when she spun around. Sarcasm bubbled up as she looped the chain of her badge around her neck and pushed him back a step. "I'm a cop. We go after people who break into buildings."

"Especially when they're lurking outside your door at the same time you're getting crank calls?"

Not so irrational, after all, eh, big guy?

Breathing out a muffled curse, John opened the door and nudged her into the hallway. "Lock it."

Maggie shoved her key into the dead-bolt lock. "You should go back to your apartment. You've already run the stairs once tonight and you're not armed."

"Lock the damn door. I'm coming with you."

By the time she twisted the key, John was already at the stairs, holding the door for her. Maggie scooted past him to peek over the railing. There was nothing to see or hear as far as she could tell, but she wasn't taking any chances. "Keep to the wall. I'll take lead."

Despite the uneven rhythm of his gait behind her, Maggie was surprised to feel John at her heels every step of the way down the stairs. The dim wattage of security lights in the stairwell limited her vision to only a few steps at a time, frustrating her need to find the man who was turning the hard-won serenity of her settled world into a nightmare.

Every time she checked a hallway and passed an empty landing, she mentally noted a *clear* report. John was right. Whoever had been outside her door was long gone or so well-hidden that she'd never find him. But she couldn't stop. She couldn't give up on the desperate idea that catching Danny in the act of stalking her would be a simple see-him, catch-him, send-him-back-to-prison operation, and she'd be able to live a normal life again.

By the time they reached the last flight of stairs without seeing so much as a pet cat moving about the building, Maggie's adrenaline was waning and she was about to give up hope of putting an end to all the weirdness happening around her. Still, her training had taught her a thorough search meant inspecting every floor so that there were no surprises once a building had been cleared.

She slowed her pace as they reached the garage level and put up a hand to warn John to stay behind her. "Let me go out first. There are plenty of places to hide down here. What are you… Let go!"

John clamped his hands around her shoulders and forced her to an abrupt stop. She shrugged free of his grasp, but her protest stopped up in her mouth when he moved past her to feel the steel door and sniff the air.

"I smell smoke."

"Where's it coming from?" She took a deeper breath and the acrid smell stung her nostrils, shifting her concern from a man she couldn't catch to the more immediate danger. She craned her neck back, looking up into the murky shadows of seven flights of stairs. "Travis."

"Don't panic yet. Door's cold." John pushed open the door to the parking garage beneath the building. "The fire can't be that big or that close."

Maggie followed him out and turned 360 degrees. Concrete, brick, cars, trucks, laundry room, storage area, elevator. She lowered her gun to her side and darted out toward the rows of vehicles. "Could it be an engine fire? I don't see any flames."

She didn't see any signs of movement either. The laundry room was empty, and a padlock on the outside of the tenants' storage lockers told her their intruder must have run up to the street, ducked under the security gate and disappeared into the night.

Maggie came back to the stairs and elevator. "Do you think the fire's outside?"

"No." John didn't look any more like a firefighter in his red running shorts than she looked like a cop in her pajamas. But there was something so methodical and focused in his movements along the wall that he inspired both confidence and an uneasy sense of pending danger. He was trusting his nose, not his eyes. He ran his hands along the bricks, traced his fingers along the seams of metal access panels and smelled the air. Maggie jumped when he snatched his fingers back as though one of the bricks had bitten him. "It's in the wall. Localized from the feel of it." He glanced from the stairwell door to the elevator, then up into the support beams over their heads. "That won't last long if it gets into the infrastructure. There are all kinds of conduits behind this wall it can travel up. Phones, power, cable, heating and AC."

"The fire will spread to the seventh floor?"

"To the whole building. I'm guessing your friend rigged it as a diversion. Crossed some wires, maybe jammed a match into the insulation."

Travis.

Maggie spotted the fire alarm beside the elevator and ran to it. But John blocked her path. "We have to wake everyone up and evacuate the building," she argued. "Travis is asleep."

"There's no hammer." He grasped both sides of the emergency fire box mounted on the wall. "One more thing Standage is responsible for that doesn't work."

"Why do you need a hammer? Hit the alarm."

Instead, he wrapped his left hand around his right fist, flexed his forearm and shouted, "Don't look!"

Maggie jerked her face away as he smashed his elbow into the glass front of the fire extinguisher box. The glass splintered and bowed. A second blow showered glass down on the concrete at his feet. She spotted drops of blood in the shattered mess. "John?"

He set the fire extinguisher on the floor and pulled out the ax behind it. "Stand back!"

"John!"

With a mighty, home-run swing, he attacked a small hollow in the wall beside one of the electrical boxes. Chunks of brick and mortar flew out and Maggie dodged out of the way of the stinging projectiles. A second blow, a third, caved in the bricks. Wisps of smoke feathered through the expanding crevice.

With a fourth blow, John hooked the ax head behind the brick facade and pulled down several chunks, revealing black char marks and smoldering insulation. "Maggie, get the extinguisher," he ordered, swinging the ax against the wall with one last blow. The whole section of bricks tumbled out, forcing John back from the avalanche.

If he was hurt or his prosthetic was damaged, he never let on. He dropped the ax and reached for the fire extinguisher, but Maggie pulled the pin and rushed past him, squeezing the trigger and spraying CO_2 foam all over the insulation, wood slats, junction box and bricks.

"You got it." John squeezed his hand around hers, urging her to release her grip. "You got it, Sarge."

Maggie's hand popped open and she let John pull the extinguisher from her shaking hands.

"Are we out of danger?" she asked. "The fire won't spread?"

He set the empty red can on the floor and brushed the dusting of mortar and grit off his hands. He turned his forearm and, for the first time, noticed the gash above his elbow. "I don't think we're catching your intruder tonight. If he didn't have us beat before, he's had plenty of time to get out of the building while we were distracted with this." He bent down and reached into the white goop she'd sprayed all over the opening. "Here's our culprit."

He wiped off the squishy remains of a cigarette butt, then sniffed it, frowned and held it up by the light next to the stairwell door.

"It's fresh." He flicked the butt back into the abyss. "Nobody's that much of an idiot to drop a lit cigarette inside a wall."

She blinked against the gases from the chemicals and pungent smoke lingering in the air. "It was deliberate?"

"Oh, yeah." Blood seeped through the fingers John clasped over his elbow. "I don't suppose you managed to tuck your phone inside your bra?"

"You're a pro at only answering the questions you want to, aren't you?" She pulled her cell from the pocket of her windbreaker. "Now what?"

"You're calling the cops and I'm calling KCFD. There are too many things going wrong around here. And I'm guessing this isn't the only one that wasn't an accident."

Chapter Seven

Maggie cut another piece of adhesive tape. "I can't believe Travis went back to sleep so fast. I figured he'd wait until the last firefighter left."

Oops, the last firefighter in the building was still sitting at her kitchen table, letting her doctor up the glass cuts on his arm. She looked up from where she knelt beside him. "Sorry."

"Pretty exciting night for a ten-year-old, huh?"

"A little too exciting if you ask me. That was nice of your friends to let him climb inside the fire engine for a few minutes, though. I just hope he'll wake up in a few hours when I get him up for school."

Maggie carefully placed the tape over the gauze bandage and gathered up the first-aid supplies. She noted a couple of tiny scratches in the rod sticking out of his black shoe. Who knew what injury the collapsing wall might have caused had that leg been skin and bone. A sudden attack of weary, guilty tears made her eyes feel gritty, but she blinked them away and pushed to her feet. John Murdock had already risked so much keeping her and the rest of his country safe. And now she'd put his life in danger again because of her stupid choices and sorry past.

The kitchen tile was cold beneath Maggie's bare feet

as she crossed to the sink to throw away the soiled cotton she'd cleaned his cuts with and wash her hands.

"The cops cleared the building and the men on the first-response truck confirmed that the fire hadn't spread beyond that part of the parking garage." Maggie shivered at the deep, even sound of John's voice coming up behind her. He appeared beside her at the counter to pick up her GLOCK off the counter and dump the magazine. She watched the practiced efficiency of his long fingers opening up the firing chamber to remove the bullet there. He reloaded the bullet into the magazine and set both it and the GLOCK on top of the refrigerator. "So, are you going to tell me why you answer the door with a loaded gun?"

A chill traveled down Maggie's spine at the ominous question. She folded her arms in front of her and rubbed at the goose bumps pricking her arms. She couldn't blame him for asking. She'd been ready to shoot to kill when she'd heard the knock on the door and had come flying through the living room. He'd probably feel a heck of a lot safer if the crazy lady next door wasn't armed. But Danny and her past had never been easy to talk about, even to a qualified therapist.

She turned her head in his direction without making eye contact. "It's really late, and I think we could both use a little sleep."

But the wide chest wasn't budging. "That bastard said, 'You can't have her. She's mine or nobody's.' Now that makes it sound like this guy thinks you and I mean something to each other. And the only type of man I know who would care about something like that is an old boyfriend. Or an ex-husband."

The flinch in Maggie's shoulders apparently told John all he needed to know.

He leaned a hip against the counter to face her. And

even though he ducked his head to try to read what she was sure was an unnatural pallor to her chilled skin, she never raised her gaze above the earth, eagle and anchor logo on his T-shirt. "If that was your ex, making calls and setting fires and who knows what else, you need to call your attorney now."

How could the man who'd chased away a bone-deep chill just hours earlier make her feel so cold now? She hugged her arms tighter and nodded toward the clock on the stove. "Before three in the morning?"

"I don't mind waking him."

"Fortunately it's not your decision to make." Tipping her head to finally meet that probing gaze, she flashed him a look that she hoped would put an end to the conversation.

She spun around to retrieve her windbreaker from the back of a chair and slide her arms into the sleeves. What had she been thinking—allowing John Murdock into her home? Standing here in her pajamas? Turning to him for solace and support because a nightmare from her past resurrected itself and caught her off guard?

She needed to back off the whole idea of having a hero come to her rescue. She needed to be self-sufficient. She needed to think this through. "We can't even prove that that was Danny who called."

"Twice. In the middle of the night." He straightened from the counter, making the distance she'd tried to put between them seem insignificant.

"All he said was my name, too softly for me to identify a voice. Then some heavy breathing. And I didn't hear him speak to you. It could have been anyone." The arch of John's eyebrow told her he knew she didn't believe that. But she couldn't back down; she didn't want to admit that Danny had become a part of her life again. "And I never knew my ex-husband to smoke. He was always about being fit and working out."

"You don't have to smoke to have access to cigarettes and a lighter."

"You can't be sure it was him on the stairs either."

"He put a lot of people at risk tonight."

When the green-gold glare never wavered, she felt compelled to add, "Fine. I promise to call first thing in the morning and let my attorney know it's a possibility, okay? So just drop it."

John shrugged, his big shoulders creating a ripple effect in the kitchen's quiet atmosphere. "Like you said, it's not my decision. I can see I've overstayed my welcome."

With just a few steps, he strode through the archway and left her alone. *Alone.* With Danny out there in the world somewhere, watching, waiting for his next chance to get to her.

Maggie ran to the archway to stop him before he reached the front door. "Would you like some tea?"

So much for standing on her own two feet.

She held her breath as John halted in the shadows of the unlit room. She knew they both worked in the morning, and the hour was already late. She knew the former marine had better things to do than deal with her problems.

Maggie also knew she really didn't want to be alone right now. She'd never had an ally against Danny before, and had worked ten long years to get to the point where she didn't need one. But please, please, please, don't let John Murdock think she was such a crazy woman that she didn't appreciate his help and concern. Please let him turn around and stay until she could get these nerves worked out of her system and become a competent cop and confident woman and think on her own two feet again.

She was still holding her breath like some kind of

dumbstruck teenage girl who'd just asked the high school quarterback to the Sadie Hawkins dance when John turned around. "Tea sounds good."

It was too dark to tell if the glare had disappeared, but the quiet depth of his voice skittered like a caress against her ears. Her breath rushed out on a noisy sigh and she tiptoed back across the cool tiles to turn on the light over the stove and pick up the kettle.

Nervous energy thrummed through her veins as she filled the teakettle with fresh water. Was this relief crashing through her system? Trepidation at entertaining a grown man in the middle of the night? Anticipation of forming an alliance that could, at the very least, give her an outlet for expressing the fears she'd guarded close to her heart for so long, and, at the very most, give her an extra pair of eyes and ears to help her avoid Danny and keep her son safe? Maybe her inability to be still had to do with something else altogether—something she hadn't even allowed herself to feel for a very long time.

Awareness. Attraction. Desire.

She was so out of practice at relating to a man who wasn't a coworker or a perp, and whose age landed in the eligible range between father figure and ten-year-old that she couldn't be sure what she was feeling.

John Murdock was a fascinating mix of Jekyll and Hyde. Even if he refused to pin the ribbons and hardware to his uniform, he wore the medals he'd earned serving his country in every proud step he took. He walked on an artificial leg and had visible burn scars, but there was nothing weak or wounded about those broad shoulders and strong arms. He could be gruff and standoffish one minute, and almost possessively concerned the next. She should be afraid of a man who was bigger and stronger than she was. Yet every newly awakened cell of her body had been imprinted with the memory of what it felt like to be held by him—to be surrounded by his heat and strength, to feel secure in a way she never had before. And foolish as it might be, she longed to be held that way again.

History had taught her a bitter lesson about her inability to judge men. But tonight she was trusting another lesson she'd learned the hard way—that a man's merit shouldn't be judged by his outward appearance or his personality. Handsome charmers could be deadly. And maybe a damaged marine who showed up unannounced and uninvited on her doorstep in the middle of the night was someone she could trust.

"I figured you for a coffee drinker." She pulled out the tea tin and sorted through the bags inside. "I'm assuming you want an herbal blend at this hour. No caffeine?"

The oak chair creaked beneath his weight. "Surprise me."

Maggie opened the dishwasher and pulled out mugs and saucers. Trusting though she was willing to be, there was an unfamiliar intimacy about having a grown man in her quiet kitchen at this time of night that raised goose bumps along her skin. She set out the sugar bowl and asked if he wanted milk. Then she was back at the tea tin again, digging through it to find the precise flavor that appealed to her right now. Something to calm her ping-ponging thoughts? Or something to boost her courage? Maybe she was the one with the Jekyll and Hyde personality. She should double-check that Travis was still asleep with his ball glove. Maybe she should get dressed. Or at least brush out the sleep-rumpled hair that kept falling into her face.

"Maggie, sit."

The mug she held clattered in its saucer before she righted it with both hands. Her heart thundered in her chest. "I don't take orders like that very well. Especially from a guest in my own home."

"Fair enough. Sarge, will you sit with me, please?" The deep timbre of his voice could be downright mesmerizing when he softened it like that. "I know I'm barging into your life, and maybe I'm not welcome, but I think you need to talk."

She tucked her hair behind her ears, rubbed her damp palms over her hips and turned. A reassuring smile never quite took hold. "You're welcome here. Always."

"Sit."

John's quiet patience seemed to soothe her own rapid pulse. With a nod of acquiescence, she came to the table and pulled out a chair on the opposite side. "Where should I start?"

"Wherever you need to."

His hazel eyes glimmered gold in the dim light of the kitchen, encouraging her to open up. But she couldn't just jump into Danny Wheeler and the memories of pain and terror. So she pulled her feet up onto the seat and hugged her knees to her chest. She nodded toward the bedroom outside the archway. "I wish I had Travis's ability to fall asleep fast and stay oblivious to the world until the alarm goes off in the morning."

"That must make it easy for the tooth fairy to pay him a visit."

She nodded at the silly comment, appreciating the effort at humor, but knowing she needed to steer the conversation toward more serious matters. "I checked his cell phone. It's working just fine now. Maybe the moisture from the rain did mess with it, but I'm thinking he saw it as a way to spend some time with you. You've been a popular topic lately."

"Yeah, he asked a lot of questions before you got home

tonight—everything from timing his batting swing to wanting to know what it was like to drive a fire engine."

"He probably loved that."

"Well, I don't drive one anymore." His chest expanded with a controlled sigh. "But back in the day…"

"But you're a firefighter."

"Arson investigator. I go into a fire after the fact now." She could hear him tapping his false leg under the table. "I'm not on the front lines anymore."

"You were tonight." The regret she heard in his voice saddened her. Although she didn't see how having the brains, training and experience to do that kind of analysis and help put away criminals or prevent similar tragic accidents could be a bad thing. "Sounds a lot like detective work. I love the challenge of solving a puzzle like that. I'm hoping to make detective one day soon myself."

"Yeah?"

"Yeah. I just graduated with my degree in criminal justice in December." She shrugged her shoulders around her clasped knees. Maybe she shouldn't have revealed just how delayed she'd been about taking control of her life after the devastation of her marriage. But she suspected John had agreed to a cup of tea so he could get some facts to explain the harassing phone calls and arsonist in the building, not to trade stories. She needed to say something to alleviate his concern. She brushed a wayward strand of hair off her face and held it behind her ear. "Travis knows he could have called me at the precinct. Whether or not I'm in the middle of an investigation, they'd have gotten a message to me. I'm sorry he bothered you."

"It wasn't a bother. Compared to the way I used to live my life, it's nice to know that I can still be useful."

"Useful?" Surprised by the admission, Maggie dropped her feet to the floor and turned toward him, crossing her arms on top of the table. How could a man whose touch had blotted out her fears and whose quick action had prevented a small fire from becoming a big tragedy think he had nothing to offer? "You've taken on not one but two heroic careers. How do you figure you're not useful?"

"Is it possible the calls came from someone besides your ex-husband? I don't want to leave you exposed to more trouble because we didn't look at other possibilities. Is there something about a case you're working on now that makes you feel like you have to arm yourself at home?"

Ouch. She'd run into walls before. So it was fine for the man to come over here and question her, but if she showed any concern about him, the subject was closed. More Jekyll and Hyde. "I don't know who you used to be, John Murdock. All I know is the man you are now. And if I didn't think I could trust you, you wouldn't be here right now."

"So you let me in." She could learn a thing or two from his interrogation tactics. The man didn't mince words or waver from his goal. "But are you going to answer my question?"

Maggie exhaled a surrendering breath. If he was going to be rescuing her son and holding her in his arms and insinuating himself into their lives, she supposed she owed him some explanation. "I've been a desk officer for most of my career. Not a position where you make a lot of enemies. My chief assigned me to the Rose Red Rapist task force—sort of an internship for detective work. But I've been a part of that for only a few days."

"I imagine you could make enemies on a case as big as that." John leaned forward, seeming to assess every response she gave. Maggie drew back a few inches. "That bastard was in the papers back before I went overseas. The cops never caught him?"

She shook her head. "The crimes stopped for a while and any leads the department had went nowhere. Now he's back. There was a victim attacked with the same M.O. a week ago." Maggie fiddled with the corner of the place mat in front of her. The unsettling events these past few days struck too personal a note to be attributed to someone who didn't know her, right? Could there be another enemy out there? Was she so worried about Danny coming back into her life that she was overlooking a different threat? "I'm more support staff and investigator-in-training than a real detective yet. I blew off a reporter last night who thought I knew something insightful about the case. I don't."

"Would this Rose Red Rapist know that? Has anyone else on the task force been targeted?"

"Targeted?" The place mat crumpled between her fingers.

"Maybe your ex did send you flowers and a love letter. But an elevator mishap? Communication lines out just on our floor?" He pointed out just how personal the odd events had become. "Lines that were out until *your* phone rang at midnight?"

Her fingers fisted around the corner of the placemat. "Those things could happen anywhere, to anybody."

"If you make an excuse for one more thing—" Maggie snapped her gaze back to John and that focused intensity wouldn't let her look away again. He reached across the table and laid his fingers over her fisted hand. "Don't tell me it's nothin'. I know what scared looks like, and what a person does to cover it up. And, Sarge, you've got that look. If it's not the rape investigation, then I'm guessing it's your ex—and that it wasn't a friendly divorce."

A bubble of familiar terror stuck in her throat. Danny Wheeler wasn't something she'd talked about with anyone except her therapist and Chief Taylor. But the bubble burst with an exhale of relief that he'd guessed her secret, and her fingers relaxed and slid beneath the warmth of John's hand. "Pretty easy to figure out, huh?"

"He's the one who called tonight, isn't he?"

"I can't be sure, but I wouldn't put it past him to say something like that."

What was it about those beautiful eyes blocking out everything else but their focus on her that made her think she could trust this guy? "Can you talk about it?"

She was surprised to discover that she could.

"I married too young and I married wrong. Danny Wheeler was abusive. Very." Her fingers flinched as she spoke, but John's grip around her hand was rock-steady—the same way his arms had been when he'd held her so close. Just like before, his touch steadied her nerves and allowed her to choose her words very carefully. "That's why Chief Taylor thought I'd be a good fit for the task force. I'm a rape victim, too."

Those eyes finally blinked and looked away. She could only imagine what kind of curse or emotion that steely jaw was crushing into silence. With another blink, John looked at her again. His grip on her hand shifted. Tightened. The intimacy of the night shrank down to the graze of a callused thumb over the tender skin on the inside of his wrist. "Can you tell me about it?"

"I tried to leave him once. We had a daughter."

"Did he ever…?"

"Hurt her?" Danny had never laid a hand on their daughter. And yet… "Angel wasn't even in school yet when Danny took her. You know, to make me come back. He got drunk and passed out. By the time I got there, she'd wandered out of the motel room where he was hiding and got hit by a car."

John was observant enough to know how that accident

had turned out. "Please tell me there's something positive coming out of this story."

Maggie's fingers danced inside John's grip. The only silver lining to this story was asleep with his ball glove in the next room. "That's when I knew there was no chance at reconciliation, that even if Danny stopped drinking, I couldn't be with him again. I filed for divorce. I was moving my things out of our apartment when he…trapped me on the elevator."

John's hand squeezed painfully tight. Just as quickly, his fingers eased their grip. "I'm sorry. I'm so sorry. So you beat this bastard, right?"

In a way, she supposed she'd defeated her ex the morning she'd awoken in the hospital and decided that weekend of terror would never happen again. "I got my divorce, sent Danny to prison and had Travis all in the same year."

The stroke of John's thumb stopped. This time the curse was audible. "Travis is the product of your husband raping you?"

Maggie nodded. She reached out to hold on to John's hand with both of hers, easing his temper and rediscovering some of her own strength. "I haven't told Trav. I may never tell him. It's not like Danny wants to be a part of his life. Why tell my son he was born out of anything besides my love for him?"

"How long has Danny been out of prison?" John's fingers danced across the palm of her hand, sending a riot of goose bumps up her arm and kindling a slower, more languid heat inside.

Maggie wondered if John was finding comfort in these simple touches across the table, too. "Long enough for him to show up as a person of interest on the task force's suspect list. His term in Jefferson City ran about the same time that the Rose Red Rapist stopped his attacks here in K.C."

"Do you think he's the serial rapist?"

She'd been wondering that ever since the day of the first task force meeting when her ex's name had come up. "I never thought he'd hurt anybody but me. But I know that officers from KCPD have talked to him since he was released from prison."

"So even if he's not this Rose Red guy, he probably associates you with the police investigating him. That could explain the calls and the late-night visit."

"Isolation is a classic tactic of abusive men." She shivered at the idea Danny would have deliberately sabotaged her phone so that she couldn't have contact with anyone until he was ready to talk to her himself. She knew what she had to do. "I'll report the calls, the fire—everything—to the task force when we meet tomorrow." She glanced over at the clock on the stove. "Or rather, later this morning."

John read the clock, too, and pulled his hand away. "In the meantime, we're looking out for a man with a shaved head and tattoos."

Missing the warmth of his touch, Maggie tucked her legs up to her chest again. It was a little unnerving to realize that he'd paid such close attention to the comments she'd made during that first panic attack when he'd been moving in. Still, John was a civilian now. And as much as she appreciated his concern tonight, and how talking things through was starting to calm her fears, she knew she shouldn't ask for more from him. "*I'm* looking out for a man like that."

"Without any backup? What are they teaching at the police academy these days?" He leaned back in his chair, scrubbing his hand over the beard growth dusting his jaw. "You got a picture of this guy?"

With a wry laugh, she turned toward the bubbling sounds of the hot kettle on the stove. "Strangely enough, I didn't want to keep any."

"Do you have an address on the exterminator company he works for?"

Needing to take charge of something and move, Maggie got up to turn off the kettle before the whistle shrieked and woke Travis. "I'm sure it'll be easy to find. It's on my to-do list. I'll have a chat with Travis to remind him about staying safe, too."

"I'll have a look around the building tomorrow. Make sure I'm familiar with all the access points and exits here." She heard the chair scooting across the tile behind her and knew he was getting up. "I think I'll follow up on some of Joe's repair work, too."

"And what, check for signs of sabotage?" She poured the hot water over the tea bags in each mug before turning. "John, I'm not asking you to do anything like that."

"You worried I can't do the job?" he asked.

Why would he think… Oh. Her gaze lighted on his leg at just the wrong time, and his posture instantly changed. In the space of a heartbeat, the warmth and concern and soothing comfort he'd brought with him vanished. "I didn't mean—"

"Fine." He'd already backed through the archway and was heading through the living room. "But you get a co-worker to walk you to your car and get Standage to make sure the outside doors stay locked. Have him put up a security camera—"

"John."

Don't stand there, Maggie. Don't let him leave like this. Do it.

Maggie hurried after him. "John Murdock." The muscles in his forearm bunched beneath her hand when she stopped him at the door. With a gentle tug, she asked him to face her and read the sincerity in her eyes. "I don't doubt your abilities or your good intentions for one moment. You're a marine. Wounded or not, you're not afraid to go into battle. But this isn't your fight. I'm a cop. I'm trying to protect you." She wasn't sure if it was his arm or her fingers quivering where they still touched, but she knew she didn't want to pull away. "You don't know my ex. Danny claims he's changed. But the man I knew was violent and unpredictable. Smart, too. Sometimes, he'd just blow up and lose his temper. Those episodes were shocking and painful, but at least I knew they would end. I could recover from them and move on."

"What about the other times?"

Damn, the man was tall. And broad. And when he faced her like this, Maggie felt exposed and feminine and vulnerable. But he didn't need to know the details about Danny's traps and cruel, calculating games. He only had to be warned. "I don't want to form a neighborhood watch against Danny. He'll strike out at anyone who gets in his way. I don't want anyone else to get hurt because of me."

"Don't worry, Sarge. I'm all heroed-out. I just want to do a little poking around. Find out if anyone else around here needs to be worried about what your ex might try to pull. I'd like to know if the things happening around here are deliberate or spur-of-the-moment, and if Danny has any friends in the building."

She braced her hand at the center of his chest, petting him, gentling him, begging him to understand. "John, I'm not asking you to do anything like that."

"I'm volunteering."

"Why?"

He covered her hand with his. "Because some things are worth fighting for. Like the daughter of a fellow marine. The safety of the people where I live. The idea that a woman shouldn't have to take crap like that from any man. It doesn't matter whether it's my battle. It needs to be fought."

Some things are worth fighting for. She'd uttered the same words to Chief Taylor when he'd asked her to join the task force. The echo of that sentiment resonated deep inside her, telling her she had more in common with John Murdock than sharing the same address. "I thought you were all *heroed-out.*"

"Maybe I'd just like to be able to sleep at night."

Her gaze dropped to the clasp of their hands. "I'm sorry. I'm trying to be strong and independent. I never wanted my problems to become anyone else's."

A callused finger slipped beneath her chin and tilted her face back to his. "Would he use Travis to get to you? Like he used your daughter?"

Her silence was answer enough. John brushed a rebellious strand of copper hair off her cheek and tucked it behind her ear. And then, after a moment's hesitation and a catch of breath between them, he dipped his head and covered her mouth with his.

John's kiss was no-nonsense. There was no tentative exploration, no forceful claim. His lips moved over hers gently but surely. He smelled of smoke and dust and man, and Maggie couldn't imagine anything more empowering than answering his sensuous request. Maggie's lips parted, clung, explored with surprising welcome. Her hand drifted up to the strong line of his jaw and she tickled her sensitive palm against the soft rasp of beard stubble there. She hadn't kissed a man since Danny. Hadn't wanted to.

But she wanted this. She needed this. She'd had no idea how much she craved this intimate, human contact.

John's kiss was about trading warmth and support. It was about the surprise of the unexpected tension sizzling between them. It was about talking and listening and understanding each other in a way that only two people so wounded by life could fully comprehend.

It was a kiss that ended so abruptly that Maggie swayed on her feet.

But two strong hands were there to catch her. The room was still spinning when John leaned in to rest his forehead against hers. Her eyes popped open to look up into a sea of deep green flecked with shards of gold.

"I don't know how you're doing this to me, Sarge. I'm not ready to feel anything."

She wasn't ready to be having feelings for someone either. But ill-timed or unexpected as the tenuous emotions might be, there they were, taking root inside her. So she had no answer for him. The Marines had landed in her life, and she wasn't strong enough to keep pushing this one away.

"I'm keeping an eye on the place," he promised. "And on the two of you. Until you tell me otherwise, we're in this fight together."

Chapter Eight

"So KCPD's finest haven't been able to figure out squat yet."

He turned the black newsprint to the single lamp that illuminated the dark office and smiled at the news story in the early edition of the *Kansas City Journal*. Hot off the presses. The ink was fresh enough to smell, and if he used his imagination, the paper was still warm to the touch. He trailed his finger along each line of the story.

It started with a historical account of what had been labeled a "troubling chain" of sex crimes attributed to a single, unknown attacker. Then it went on to make mention of his latest conquest, calling her "the stepdaughter of one of Kansas City's wealthiest businessmen." Wealthy? Beautiful? Entitled? Then the woman deserved to be taken down a peg. He'd done the city a great service.

The woman's injuries got less comment than the discussion of her stepfather's assets and a lame quote about how a "substantial reward will be offered" for any solid leads on the attack. The story mentioned Fairy Tale Bridal Shop and a street name, but there wasn't even a description of a vehicle or alleged attacker mentioned.

For all the fine writing, there really wasn't a lot of meat to the story. There was more talk about the commissioner announcing a new task force than there was about anything else. It was a weak story. Far too weak. He read few facts beyond the names of the police officers, advisers and support staff assigned to the investigation.

One. Two. Three women's names were listed. He stroked his finger across each one. These women had no power over him. They couldn't touch him, couldn't hurt him. And this one woman, Maggie Wheeler—make that *Sergeant* Maggie Wheeler—had the nerve to brag that she'd been the first one to break any kind of lead on the case when she'd gotten the witness to open up to her.

A familiar, predatory urge stirred in his loins.

Maggie Wheeler. Worthless bitch. She only thought she'd gotten something useful from her interview with the blonde woman.

There was something extraordinarily satisfying about outsmarting the entire police department, about putting these women in their place. His nostrils flared as he breathed in deeply and savored the triumph coursing through his veins.

"Not a clue," he gloated. "Not one, single clue."

Yet a niggling bit of annoyance whispered in his ear. He hadn't done enough to assuage the hurt yet. The story wasn't important enough to make the front page. *He* wasn't important enough to be taken seriously. The Gabriel Knight article was buried on the second page between a political cartoon and an advertisement for a local theater.

"That's a good thing." The voice in his head tried to reason with the rage brewing inside him. *"You can't hide in the shadows any longer if you're plastered all over the front page. You made a mistake, had a moment of weakness. But you're better than that. You can control this."*

That's right. He was in control. No beautiful damn woman would ever make a fool of him again.

He reached the end of the column and saw that the ar-

ticle was continued on the last page of the section. The
last page? He hadn't even merited a proper headline and
now he was just a to-be-continued in the local paper? His
breath constricted in his lungs and he rubbed at his chest.

"Ah, hell." He'd smeared a black mark across his clean
T-shirt.

Angrily, he shot to his feet and tossed the newspaper
onto the chair. He peeled off the shirt en route to the nearest bathroom and folded it into a neat rectangle before
dropping it into the bag beside the sink.

"Easy," the voice warned. *"You don't want anyone to
know the truth."*

"Shut up." He railed against the face staring back from
the mirror over the sink. He was a handsome enough man,
wasn't he? He had a job. He'd made a whole damn career
for himself. People should respect him. But it wasn't good
enough. *He* wasn't good enough.

"That's not true," the voice was quick to argue. *"You've
taken a few hits, but you're a good man. Take a deep
breath. Get a grip before you get yourself into trouble
again."*

Get a grip?

He slowly opened his fisted hands and grimaced at the
black ink staining every finger. He was dirty. An abhor-
rent sourness churned in his gut and he nearly retched.

His own thoughts, as well as the voice, went silent as
he turned on the hot water and pumped palmfuls of soap
into his hands. He scrubbed and scrubbed at the ink until
his fingers were clean and the skin was pink. He splashed
more soap and water on his face, then reached into his bag
for a bottle of hand sanitizer and a clean shirt.

He wasn't sure how many minutes passed before the
fog of his obsession cleared from his brain and he heard a
knock at the bathroom door. He froze at the sound. How

long had that person been listening in? How long had he
been in here, washing away the filth and the rage?

"It's time."

His voice sounded surprisingly normal as he answered
the summons to the morning meeting. "I'll be right there."

"I SEE WE MADE THE PAPER." Spencer Montgomery walked
through the conference room door and circled the table,
placing a copy of the *Kansas City Journal* in front of each
task force member. Maggie opened her copy to the page
he indicated. "So, in addition to having our plates full
with this investigation, we all need to watch what we say
to Gabriel Knight."

A quick skim through the article did little to alleviate
Maggie's guilt. "I never said Miss Austin's name, I swear.
He guessed the victim's name. His question about the in-
terview at the hospital caught me off guard, and whatever
I said or did was enough to confirm the guess."

"Relax, Wheeler." The red-haired detective sat at the far
end of the table. "Knight talked to all of us. I just hope this
doesn't have anything to do with those incidents at your
building you reported. I'm not thrilled to see our names
listed there."

Annie Hermann stuffed the last of the muffin she was
eating into her mouth and grabbed her newspaper. "We
are?"

"The information was in KCPD's official press release."
Although Spencer Montgomery's words were meant to
be reassuring, Maggie could tell by the pinch of a frown
between his brows that he wasn't pleased. "I'd pay good
money to keep our investigation out of the papers. Ano-
nymity would make our job a little easier. Witnesses and
informants will be more reluctant to come forward if they
think they'll see their name in the paper. And if our perp

gets any sign that we're onto him, it could drive him un-derground again."

"Or make him even smarter about how to cover up his crimes," his partner, Nick Fensom, suggested before taking a long drink of his coffee.

Kate Kilpatrick, looking enviously fresh and stylish so early in the morning, offered another warning. "The pub-licity could play in to his power trip as well, making him even more dangerous. The *Journal*'s readers aren't just here in Kansas City. Its circulation is statewide. And if the story gets picked up on the wire and internet, we'll be giving this guy national attention. A lot of people are going to be following every move we make."

Just like a white exterminator's van and unseen eyes had followed *her?*

Maggie stopped typing her notes as her thoughts drifted back to her late-night conversation with John Murdock. He suspected her work on the Rose Red Rapist investigation might be the cause of the unwanted calls and weird events that had rattled any sense of security she'd fought so hard for. Was it possible that a woman who'd purposely flown under society's radar for so long now had more than a vi-cious ex-husband for an enemy?

She hoped he'd be home when she got there tonight. She wanted to be there when he went poking around the building to find some sign of last night's intruder, or evi-dence of any of the building's breakdowns being delib-erate. Not just because she needed those answers to plan out the best strategy for keeping Travis safe, but because having a friend like John in her corner made *her* feel safe. He made her feel a few other things, too, but she wasn't any more ready to acknowledge and explore those feelings than John claimed he was.

When her attention came back to the task force meeting, Spencer was still voicing his concerns. "We're under a microscope now. If we make mistakes, it'll hurt our credibility."

Nick Fensom chimed in. "And if our leads are publicized, that allows the perp to stay a step ahead of us."

Dr. Kilpatrick jotted a note in her planner. "I'll call Mr. Knight with an official statement, and explain the risks of giving the case too much coverage."

"He'll plead the First Amendment, say the public has a right to know." Nick scowled.

"And I'll argue victims' rights," Kate countered. "There's a fine line we have to walk with the press. We want Kansas City to be aware of Rose Red, but we don't want the city paralyzed by fear of more attacks. Nor do we want to hinder any victim's recovery or jeopardize any future prosecution."

"You're on Gabe Knight, then," Spencer agreed. He sorted through the printouts in the notebook in front of him. Something among the meticulous records diverted his attention.

Maggie typed in Dr. Kilpatrick's assignment to talk to Gabriel Knight at the *Journal*. She was sitting with her fingers poised over the keyboard to input the team's next directive when she realized Detective Montgomery was waiting for her to look up and make eye contact. Had she missed something? "What?"

Was that Spencer Montgomery's version of a smile? "I read your report of your interview with Bailey Austin. Impressive for a first-timer to get her to open up like that."

"Thank you," she answered hesitantly. The lead detective would clean up in a poker game. She couldn't tell if that was amusement or if she was in some kind of trouble for overstepping the bounds of a relative intern. "I think she just wanted somebody to listen to her."

"Possibly." So no pat on the back after all. "But when Chief Taylor said our prime witness could identify her rapist by smell, I was hoping for something more useful than pickles."

Maggie set her laptop on the table. "That's what she said the smell reminded her of—pickles."

Annie Hermann snapped her fingers and reached down to pick up the oversize bag she carried. She pulled out a bent file marked with the crime lab stamp. "Pickles would make sense with the preliminary results from the lab."

"How's that?" Nick wadded up the paper cup from the coffee he'd been drinking and shot it into the trash can beside the door. "That our perp likes to snack on gherkins and dills?"

"No, smart-ass." Annie handed the wrinkled report off to Detective Montgomery. "Vinegar. The lab found traces of vinegar in the victim's panties."

Dr. Kilpatrick sat forward in her chair. "That's not good."

"Pickles have vinegar in them, don't they?" Nick asked.

"Yes." Maggie already knew that Dr. Kilpatrick's concern wasn't about food. Maybe it was a good thing that Bailey Austin hadn't remembered every detail of her attack. "Women used to use vinegar as a cleansing agent after sex. There was an old wives' tale that it worked as a contraceptive."

"You think our perp is some old fart?" Nick asked. "How do you explain the physicality of the attacks, then?"

The CSI across from him groaned. "Listen, Mr. Neanderthal, our guy doesn't have to be old-school to use vinegar. Wives' tale or not, it's an effective way to clean up traces of DNA off the vic. That's why we haven't been able to find any kind of scientific ID on this guy. We can't even tell you what kind of condom he uses because any trace we manage to pull has been compromised."

"He disinfected her? After..." Nick swore under his breath. "If that bastard comes after either one of my sisters—"

"Relax, Nick." Spencer cooled his partner's outburst. "I think we're all in agreement that we can't get this guy off the streets soon enough."

"But we're back to square one," Nick argued.

Maggie piped up shyly, even though she hadn't been asked her opinion directly. "Miss Austin said she came to in an abandoned office building—either under construction, or being renovated or torn down. Could we start a search for properties like that in the area where she was abducted?"

Pike Taylor nodded toward the dog at his feet. "Hans and I are game."

"There's no evidence the assault took place in that area," Spencer pointed out, "only the abduction."

Nick looked at his partner. "You got any other leads, Spence? We need to try something."

"Wheeler's plan it is." After a moment to consider their limited options, Spencer agreed, closing his notebook. "Let's go pull construction and demolition orders for a six-block radius around the abduction site near that bridal shop. Pike, you'll get a search team together? Remember, nothing too big—we don't want to raise this guy's suspicions."

"Will do."

Wheeler's plan? Maggie dipped her head to hide her smile as a fledgling sense of pride and accomplishment swelled inside her. She could be a detective. She could help these victims.

But there was little opportunity to savor the success

of her idea. Without any official dismissal, the meeting seemed to be ending. Everyone at the table was getting up, gathering their things, moving with a purpose. It was business as usual at the Fourth Precinct, and Maggie was starting to feel less like the gatekeeper between KCPD and the public, and more like an integral part of the task force.

Detective Montgomery opened the door. "Annie, see if your lab can at least identify what brand of vinegar it is and find out where our perp could have bought the stuff."

"Could be a long list."

"It'd be more than we've got now."

Kate Kilpatrick filed past the red-haired detective. "I'll pull the files from ten years ago and start reading through them. See if there's any mention of vinegar or empty buildings in the victim statements."

Maggie was the last one to reach the door. "What should I do?" she asked. "Besides copy details of the meeting to everyone."

Detective Montgomery thought for a moment, then closed the door behind them. "Get with the doc on those old files and line up some interviews with the previous victims. You got Bailey Austin to open up, maybe you can get one of them to remember something more, as well."

"Yes, sir." Feeling more like the detective she aspired to be than she'd ever felt before, Maggie quickly crossed the floor back to her front desk station across from the third-floor elevators.

She spent some time at her desk, copying the meeting notes into an email and sending them out to Chief Taylor and the task force members. She verified the duty log for the day, then agreed to cover the desk for Officer Allen's fifteen-minute break so that he could manage the front on his own while she went upstairs to Dr. Kilpatrick's office to work on the victim interviews with her.

Maggie was giving a visitor directions when the elevator doors opened. Her training to be the precinct's first line of defense as well as its first opportunity to welcome guests had her automatically turning to identify the elevator's occupants.

She never heard the woman's thank-you or saw her walk away. Maggie's pulse was thundering in her ears, and her vision had narrowed down to the shiny bald pate and deceptively handsome face of Daniel Gable Wheeler.

He was coming this way, sauntering across the marble floor in his tan work coveralls. His laser-blue eyes locked onto hers, and he was smiling. He grinned that charming smile that had once knocked the teenage Maggie off her feet as though the abuse, the threats, the rape and that fire last night had never happened.

Run. Scream. Fight. Do something.

Danny rested his elbows on the counter and laced his tattooed fingers together. "Hey, baby. The guy downstairs said I needed to sign in here and get a visitor's pass."

Any civilized greeting escaped her. "You can't be here."

"Sure I can, Mags. Where do I sign?" The words carved into his knuckles—*LOVE, HATE*—were a mocking testament to their relationship, and gave graphic emphasis to the damage those powerful hands had done. "I volunteered to come in for questioning on the Rose Red Rapist case. I'm meeting with a Detective Fensom. I'm all about proving my innocence."

Fat chance. The sooner she got him away from her and out of the building, the better.

"Fine. When's your appointment?" She lay the clipboard and a visitor's pass on top of the counter and reached for the phone. While Danny signed the registry, she checked the duty log for Nick Fensom's extension. "I'll get you set up in an interview room and let him know you're here."

The hand that said *LOVE* shot over the counter and grabbed her wrist. Maggie instantly tensed and tried to pull away. Her struggle was subtle and brief. What if someone else on the floor saw her unable to properly defend herself? What if she went ballistic and created an incident that shouldn't have to happen? And why couldn't she decide what to do? It wasn't the offense of his unwanted touch that stunned her, but that the bruising strength still felt so familiar. Had she come such a short way in ten years that Danny's touch could still make her brain and backbone shut down like this?

"I'm being friendly here, Mags. And I don't even get a hello? I thought I'd at least earn a little credit for helping KCPD with the biggest case they've had in years." He leaned in for a more intimate whisper. "Actually, I could care less about anyone else here. I saw your name in the paper—read that this was your investigation. Now I understand why you sicced those uniformed officers on me at work to get an alibi for the last attack. You're moving up in the world. I'm proud of you, baby. I'm here to help you."

If he'd showed her anything but that sincerity in his eyes, she might have cowered. But some out-of-practice instinct that warned her never to believe what those blue eyes said finally kicked in. She could do the hushed intensity thing, too. "Danny, let go of me now or I'll throw you in a jail cell instead of an interview room. There are thirty cops working on this floor at any given time. If you try anything, all I have to do is say the word and they'll be here to back me up. So let go."

With an arch of one dark eyebrow, he eased his grip and she pulled away. While Danny put his hands up and retreated a step, Maggie put the call in to Nick.

A few minutes later, Maggie led Danny into an interview room and closed the door. "Detective Fensom is taking an important call right now. He'll be here as soon as he can." She knew standard procedure was to offer an uncuffed, voluntary interviewee a cup of coffee or glass of water, but she had no such niceties to offer her ex. It was all she could do to point to a chair. "Have a seat."

She waited until his butt was firmly planted in the chair before heading for the door. But escaping from Danny had never been easy.

"I saw your new boyfriend at the ballpark."

Maggie halted with her hand on the doorknob. "So you *were* there watching my son."

"I was waiting for you." He made his appearance sound like a romantic gesture. "I figured you'd come pick up the kid. Didn't know you'd have a boy toy to come do it for you instead."

No argument about Travis being *their* son. No remorse about driving away and leaving a child all alone after dark. No indication that he even remembered the daughter he'd taken to keep Maggie from divorcing him, and then allowed to wander into traffic and be hit by that car.

Angel's death had been the incentive to plot her escape from their marriage. Danny had punished her within an inch of her life the night he'd caught her on the elevator leaving him. Keeping Travis safe gave her the incentive to turn the doorknob. Years of training and therapy and healing gave Maggie the strength to believe Danny could never punish her again unless she let him.

"I'll guard the door from the outside until Detective Fensom gets here."

"I can see how ol' Peg Leg would make a good babysitter."

Maggie froze at the offhand comment. The logical decision to get away warred with the emotional need to put

Danny in his place, to teach him a lesson, to best him somehow for saying something so crude about the man she was falling in love with.

Before that revelation could fully register, Maggie pulled the door shut to hear Danny's next snide comment. "But he ain't all there, baby. He can't give it to you the way I can."

She wasn't the one who was going to be forced out of a room at her own workplace. Task force or not, Danny Wheeler had to go. Maggie stepped away from the door and faced him. "Get out. Unless you plan to confess to stalking me at my apartment and setting a fire in the basement, you need to leave."

"I've got no idea what you're talking about, baby." His blue eyes hooded with an expression she supposed was his version of longing and regret. "We were once so good together, Mags. That's all I want. Like I said, I'm sober now. I'm holdin' down a job." He leaned across the table and reached out to her. "On our wedding day you promised you'd love me forever. I haven't forgotten those vows. I want to get back to the way things were when everything was right between us."

Maggie ignored the outstretched hand. "Nothing was ever right, Danny. I was just too afraid to realize I could have something better."

His fingers curled into a fist and he pushed to his feet. "And you think screwing old Sergeant Hopalong is better than being with me?"

How had she ever thought Danny Wheeler was hero material? Shaking her head, she turned for the door. "Leave, Danny. Now. Or I'll call your P.O. and tell him you violated your restraining order. I'll tell Detective Fensom that you had to reschedule your meeting."

She never reached the doorknob. Danny grabbed her by

the collar and swung her around to slam her up against the
wall. "You uppity bitch. *I* tell you when we're done talkin'."
His hand curled around her throat, and his hips butted up
against hers, anchoring her in place with her toes barely
touching the floor. But her hands were free. She clawed
at his wrist but was rewarded with a tighter choke hold
and his hot breath in her face. "I'm trying to be reason-
able here. You won't meet with me when I ask nicely, so
we have to have this conversation any way I can."

Rage spiraled up and twisted with the instinctive need
to free herself. *Think. Take him down. Do it!*

Danny was the same person he'd been ten years ago.
Maggie was not.

Twisting her legs free and fighting for breath, Maggie
thrust her palm up under his nose, hard enough to feel the
pop inside. Danny instantly loosened his grip and grabbed
his bloody nose. "You stupid, stupid—"

Maggie sucked in a reviving gulp of air, pulled her gun
and put it to his throat, backing him up until he hit the
table and the steel legs screeched across the floor. "Keep.
Your. Hands. Off. Me."

Just as quickly as the attack had come, Danny's outburst subsided. His warm blood dripped on her fingers
and he started to laugh. Holding one hand up in surrender, he ignored the threat of the gun pressing into his neck
and pulled a bunch of tissues out of the box on the table
to dab at his nose. "Man, how I love that Irish temper of
yours. So much passion there. Nobody ever could control
that fire but me."

Control her? "Oh, my God."

Stunned by how thoroughly she'd just lost it, horrified
to think she'd sunk to the same gut-level violence that
Danny thrived on, Maggie pulled her gun away from the
imprint she'd left on his throat. She'd just earned a college

degree that had trained her to outthink rather than just react to a suspect like this. And outthink him was exactly what she intended to do.

He was still laughing when she grabbed him by the front of his coveralls and put him facedown on the table. "Turn around, Danny. Hands behind your back. You have any weapons on you? Anything sharp or dangerous?" After patting down his pockets, she handcuffed his wrist to the table and pushed him back down into the chair. "You're looking at assault on a police officer and violating a restraining order."

He grinned up at her. "You need my help to solve this case, Mags. I have friends on the street. I hear things."

"I don't need anything from you." She opened the door again, swung it wide so that any and everybody who walked down this hallway could see the man she'd handcuffed there. Not that she had any intention of staying. She met Danny's smile with the sternest, strongest look she could manage. "Don't you ever talk about John Murdock like that again. A woman would be lucky to have him love her. He's more of a man than you'll ever think about being."

"John, is it? And you're defending him? So it *is* personal."

She shook her head, remembering how impossible it was to reason with him, and stepped out into the cleaner air of the hallway. "Goodbye, Danny."

Lawrence Boyle was strolling down the hallway, peeking into each open doorway he walked past. Maggie sidestepped him when he approached, but he moved with her, blocking her path. "Ma'am?" He greeted her with a smile, with his hands held up in front of him to show he meant her no harm. "I was looking for Danny? The guy at the front desk said he was back here."

"In there."

"Whoa, dude, your nose." Deciding her personal desire to leave Danny as far behind as possible was secondary to leaving two former felons together and unguarded, Maggie reluctantly waited against the wall opposite the open door. Danny's boss turned his thick neck to ask her about the handcuffs. "Is he under arrest?"

Maggie hooked her thumbs into her utility belt and looked him straight in the eye. "You should go back to the waiting area, Mr. Boyle." She eyed the front of his jumpsuit for a visitor's tag. "You need to sign in."

"But he said he was only going to be half an hour." Boyle faced her fully to plead his case. "I've got my van parked downstairs. We've got a job to get to."

Danny pulled out another tissue to wipe the blood from his face. "It's okay. I may be a little longer, Lawrence. I have business to attend to."

"Yeah, I know what kind of business you're interested in." Maggie put a hand on Boyle's shoulder to keep him from entering the room. Although she felt him stiffen inside his coveralls at her silent command, thankfully, he was more willing to cooperate than Danny had been. With a nod, he promised to stay put and she released him. "Seriously, Danny? Breaking the law right here at the police station? What's the good of me giving an ex-con a break and hiring you when you go and get yourself into trouble again? And over a woman?"

"She's hot when she's all fired up and in charge, isn't she?" Danny seemed oblivious to his friend's frustration and her revulsion at the worthless compliment. "Nobody else will ever love you the way I do, Mags."

Lord, she hoped not.

"Everything okay here?" Maggie masked her sigh of relief at Nick Fensom's arrival, and channeled the raw energy coursing through her into the white-knuckled grip she had on her belt. Danny and Lawrence Boyle might top Fensom in height, but there was a cagey, badgerlike intensity about the stocky detective that made both men sit up straight and retreat a step. "I thought I asked only one of you to come in for questioning. I don't like a party."

Maggie was glad for the backup, but prayed her relief wasn't flooding her cheeks with heat. "Your appointment is in Interview Room D. Just so you know, Danny Wheeler is my ex-husband and coming within fifty yards of me is a violation of his restraining order."

Nick eyed the duo in matching coveralls before dismissing her. "I'll have a personal conversation with his parole officer, Sergeant. You get back to work."

"You interested in her, too?" Danny taunted from inside the room. "Come on, Mags, you're *my* wife, remember?"

Nick grabbed the door and flicked a thumb over his shoulder, warning Boyle out of his way. "You, out. You, shut up." Turning his attention to Danny, Nick closed the door.

The squeaky soles of Lawrence Boyle's shoes told Maggie he was hurrying to catch up with her. But she hadn't expected him to latch on to her arm or for her swerving release to be so obvious. She clamped her mouth shut and waited for the bleach-haired exterminator to speak.

"Sorry, Mrs. Wheeler. When Danny said he was in a position to do the cops a favor, I thought it was a good thing. I didn't know he was coming here to hit on you." *Hit on her?* Oh, the irony of that cliché. But those bug eyes were round and dark and smiling with good intentions. So she clamped her mouth shut and let him finish. "But Danny's a good worker. My business is expanding and I could really use his help. If Danny gets released again, I promise I'll keep him in line."

Impossible.

No one could keep Danny Wheeler in line.

No one could keep him out of her life.

Maggie saw the blood staining the sleeve of Boyle's coveralls and knew it had come from her hand. She hid her palm against her thigh and changed course to head for the bathroom. "Excuse me, I need to clean up."

Any extra confidence that the task force meeting had built inside her was gone. By the time she got inside the john, away from ex-felons and fellow cops, her knees were shaking so badly she had to grip the edge of the sink to keep them from collapsing.

After ten years Danny could still take her back to that place of insecurity and terror in an instant. She wasn't ready to be a detective. She wasn't ready to take a chance on a new relationship. She wasn't in any shape to be much good to anyone else as long as Danny could get to her like this.

Because until she could get a handle on the fear, the anger and the paranoia and second-guessing they inspired, she wasn't even any good to herself.

JOHN'S BOOTS CRUNCHED over the melted plastic and metal bits of the Wilson Irrigation Supply Company's collapsed roof. He'd replaced his ball cap with a hard hat, and his ax and fire hose with a flashlight and a computerized clipboard.

He saw the sweep of Meghan Taylor's flashlight coming up behind him before he heard her voice. "What does it look like to you, John?" She'd shed the heavy weight of her coat and breathing gear, but still wore her helmet, boots and overalls. The pale hair sticking to the sweat at her temples indicated she hadn't been home to get any sleep since yesterday's alarm. "Hazmat cleared the place of any toxic chemicals, but the rest of this place looks like a total wipe to me."

He followed her glance up to the skeletal walls and twisted metal shelves of what had once been a storage facility for miles of irrigation pipe. He agreed with her danger assessment of the surviving structure. "What's left is going to have to come down before they can do any rebuilding."

"I know they've lost a ton of inventory with this fire, but if they're going to claim it for insurance, I want to make sure it wasn't deliberate."

He nudged aside the mucky layer of water and ash with the toe of his boot and aimed his flashlight at the charred remains of an exposed wiring box. "I haven't seen any pour patterns that indicate the fire was intentionally set. But we might have a case for old age and negligence. It's a good thing your team turned off the gas feed or we'd be looking at an explosion instead of a slow burn. That junction box had probably been sparking and smoldering for days before it ignited."

John took a couple more measurements and entered his notes while Meghan climbed through the warehouse's wreckage with him. This warehouse was probably about the same 1930s vintage as The Corsican, the building where he and the Wheelers and an odd assortment of retirees and recluses lived. He wondered how many upgrades there had been as superficial and cosmetic as this place. While the fire department's visit last night had given him a plausible excuse to check on his neighbors and put together a list of all the building's recent mishaps and repairs that could be attributed to the decaying structure and quick, less-than-stellar fixes by Joe Standage, he was having less and less doubt that Maggie's problems hadn't been caused by age or accident.

"You okay?" Meghan asked, pulling him from his thoughts.

John dismissed her concern. "This just reminds me of another antique that needs to be fixed."

"I heard you had a small fire in your building last night."

"Yeah, a cigarette butt caught some old insulation wrapping on fire. We put it out with an extinguisher before the crew from Station 15 ever got there."

"We?" Meghan asked.

Two years ago—hell, even two days ago—John would have been more concerned about helping Meghan over a pile of rubble that had been knocked down to prevent it from collapsing on the firefighters who'd been fighting the blaze through the night. At the last second, he held out his hand to balance her on the climb down toward the exit. "A neighbor lady and I discovered it."

"But you don't think the fire was an accident?" He released her hand as soon as they hit solid ground.

"I'm beginning to think The Corsican is a death trap."

Meghan scoffed at his doomsday pronouncement. "Come on, I know you. I know you checked the inspections and building codes before you ever moved into the place."

She was right, he *had* made sure The Corsican met city safety codes before signing the lease. "Let me rephrase that. It's not the building that has issues—it's some freak who's trying to bring the place down around us."

"Why? What else has happened?"

It felt like a violation of trust to share any of the sick details about Maggie's disastrous marriage, even with a longtime friend like Meghan Taylor. "It's personal," was the only explanation he offered. "I need to do a little more poking around before I figure out exactly what's going on there."

He was surprised at how readily Meghan accepted his answer, and at how vehement she was about supporting his concern. "If you need anything, you put my number on speed dial. Or call the station. I haven't forgotten how you were there for me when that arsonist was setting fires in Kansas City, and I seemed to be in the middle of all of them."

"Gideon Taylor was there for you," John corrected her.

"The man I love, my boys and my best friend—" she squeezed his arm to emphasize his importance on that list "—were there for me. That's how I got through it, John. I owe you." She patted his arm and moved on ahead of him. "You call, whether it's another fire or anything else. We'll do whatever we can to help."

"Thanks, boss. I'll keep that in mind."

By mutual consent, they changed direction and headed outside to where Dean Murphy and the rest of the Station 23 crew were rolling up hoses and stowing gear. Before they hit asphalt and the jokes and shouts of the crew, Meghan stopped in front of him and turned. "I've been worried about you, John. You seem different. A heck of a lot more introspective. And here I thought it was me, that I made coming back to work uncomfortable for you. But if you've got something you're dealing with, maybe some issue with this neighbor lady you mentioned, then I won't worry so much. Unless you need me to. I don't make you uncomfortable anymore, do I?"

John looked down into the eyes of a friend. And even though there were certainly hints of regret and might-have-beens lingering inside him, the sharp pangs of unrequited love had truly dulled. His thoughts were centered on another woman now. One who just might need him the way he was beginning to need her and her son.

"No." The answer felt more honest than he'd expected.

"Yo, Big John!" John groaned at the taunt from Dean. "You know you miss this. Why don't you get your old bones on over here and show us you can still haul all this equipment."

"You're just trying to get out of work, Dean. I *am* old enough to be smarter than you and have your games figured out."

The younger man laughed and took a few more good-natured gibes from the rest of the crew before they all went back to finishing up the job at hand.

"You *do* miss it, don't you," Meghan observed. "Being in the middle of the action?"

"I get paid more than he does, and my muscles won't ache at the end of the day." Not from lifting the heavy hoses and gear at any rate. "Besides, I've seen more *action* than any man needs to."

"John, are you happy to be home?"

That was the million-dollar question, wasn't it?

Leaving it unanswered, he opened the door of his truck and tossed his hard hat and clipboard inside. "I'd better get back to the station and get my report written up. My boss is a real stickler for gettin' the job done fast and right."

Meghan smiled at the friendly jab but didn't back away from her concern. "If you need more time—to recover from your injuries or adjust to the new job or get better acquainted with the neighbor lady—"

"Are you matchmaking?"

"Do I need to?"

He climbed inside behind the wheel. "I'll see you back at the station."

Chapter Nine

A couple hours later, John was sitting in his office, pulling up the layout of the Wilson warehouse on his computer to add to his KCFD report. Although he'd bagged up some of the toasted wiring to be analyzed at the state fire lab, his preliminary findings were that the fire was accidental.

He brushed his fingertip over the top of the mouse and eyed the public building links on the screen in front of him. How hard would it be to pull up the blueprints on The Corsican—to double-check what should be in that building compared to what was actually there, and find out who had access to the building to perform inspections or maintenance on phone lines and elevator wires? Just how far should he go, following his instincts about there being something very wrong about the old building? Did one kiss, battling a fire together and a late-night heart-to-heart make him Maggie Wheeler's protector? How much of the lurking sense of pending danger surrounding Maggie was him trusting his gut? And how much was just a lost man without a purpose seeing enemies where none existed?

And was there something to Meghan's teasing about the *neighbor lady?* Was his brain still so fogged up with war and loss and recovery that he was missing something his station captain could see that he couldn't?

A soft knock at his door diverted his attention. "John?" Meghan pushed open the door. "You have a visitor."

"I do?"

Meghan stepped aside to usher in Maggie Wheeler. In that moment, John knew that his feelings for his boss were a thing of the past. He stood as the red-haired cop stepped into his office. Meghan's sunny blond hair faded into a pleasant memory as his pulse kicked into overdrive at the impact of Maggie's copper-haired beauty.

But the pale cast to the skin beneath her freckles tempered the rush of hormones. She stood tall and strong, a poster image for serving and protecting with her navy blue uniform, Kevlar and badge. But there was a searching request in those deep green eyes and a nervous fluttering of fingers through the wisps of escaping curls at her temple and nape.

"Sarge?" Meghan disappeared from the room and closed the door as he circled the desk. "What is it? Did something happen to Travis?"

She shook her head, alleviating that fear at least. "I saw Danny today. He came to the police station."

John guided her to a chair and shut the blinds on the office door. He brushed his hand across her shoulder as he perched on the edge of his desk facing her. Maybe he was offering comfort, or maybe he needed the feel of her strength and warmth for himself—a tangible reassurance that she was okay. "I thought you had a restraining order."

Maggie shot to her feet, avoiding both his touch and making eye contact. She dusted her fingers over the empty shelves behind his desk. "He had a legal way around it. He's a person of interest in the task force's investigation case. Detective Fensom wanted him to come in."

John stayed put, letting her pent-up energy carry her around the room. He couldn't imagine what kind of courage it required, and what kind of terror it caused, to come face-to-face with the man who'd raped and beaten her and stolen her child from her—a man she should have been able to trust. Protective anger fired through his blood, making it difficult to keep his own voice calm. "I'm guessing the investigation wasn't the real reason he agreed to help."

"Who knows? He could use some good karma with the police department, but...who knows?"

Beginning to understand her need to pace, John followed her to the bookshelf. Again he tried to touch her, but she crossed her arms and moved away. It was then that he saw the bruises on her wrist, the five purpling dots of violence that indicated Danny had put his hands on her.

Ah, hell. The marks were there beneath her collar, too. Double hell.

John pushed his fist against his mouth, bottling up his curse. Although he thought he could understand why Maggie might not want him touching her right now, he seethed at the idea that this wasn't the first time Danny Wheeler had hurt her.

Maybe sensing his growing rage—hell, maybe avoiding it—she abruptly changed the topic. "You don't have a single decoration in here. What about a picture of your sister? Do you have one with the two of you together? I know, you could put your medals and ribbons in a shadow box and hang them on the wall right next to your investigator certification. Or maybe frame your honorable discharge. You'd be doing this big, empty wall a favor. Showing off your accomplishments isn't bragging, John. It's just a statement of fact."

"Sarge... Maggie." He was stupefied by the sudden lightness of her tone but wasn't buying the "everything's hunky-dory now" attitude one bit. He moved in closer but didn't touch. "You didn't come here to decorate my office. When you ramble on like that, I know something's wrong. Why are you here?"

She turned to face him, eyeing his chest like she wanted to be there. He breathed deeply to conquer the urge to pull her into his arms. He squeezed his hands into tight fists down at his sides when she reached up to fiddle with the collar of his shirt—adjusting it, smoothing it, touching that one little corner of cotton knit like she was afraid to act on the need in her eyes…like she just might be afraid of him.

"Talk to me, Sarge. How do I make this right for you?"

She looked up at him then—and he was certain that green would forever be his favorite color.

Maggie pulled her hand from his shirt, denying him even that little bit of contact. But her brave, beautiful eyes never once looked away. "I want to go with you to check out our building. Now. As soon as you can get off work. If there's any way we can do it before I have to pick up Travis, that'd be great." He was ready to answer yes, but she had more to say. "I need to get ahead of this mess, John. I'm tired of just reacting. I'm at a disadvantage. I need to take control. I want to know for sure whether Danny has been in the building, and if he's responsible for any of the weird stuff that's been going on. I need to find out if there's any more crazy in store for me and the people who live there."

Her fingertips brushed against his fists and something like relief, acceptance—need—sparked between them at the shy request. John opened his hands and laced his fingers together with hers, holding on tight. It was a welcome, a promise. The trust in that simple gesture cracked open something cold and doubting that had encircled his heart.

And then he felt the grip of her fingers squeeze around his knuckles, holding on just as tightly to him.

"THAT AIN'T GOOD."

Maggie swung her flashlight around to peer into the storage unit where John had stopped. *Her* storage unit.

She curled her fingers through the chicken wire that lined the open frame of the door. Her heart plummeted to a place as dank and dark as the brick walls and wooden framework around her.

Those were her things inside the modest 6 x 6 cubby, recessed like so many others into the basement walls of The Corsican. There was Travis's tricycle she hadn't been able to part with, the collection of baseball bats that got bigger and heavier with every year and the high chair she might never need again but had been too sentimental over to part with.

That was her card table and folding chairs, set up as though someone was expecting company down here. There were her winter clothes, out of their boxes and draped over the chairs as though someone had been trying them on or sorting through them.

And then there were the pictures. Not *her* pictures. Pictures of her in shades of gray from a dozen newspapers. Taped all over the back wall. There was the task force article from the morning *Journal* that mentioned her name. There was a photo of her taken when she'd earned her sergeant's stripes. Every other officer who'd earned a rank that year had been cut out of the group picture. And there were others. A yellowed, faded image of her and Danny's engagement announcement from a naval base newsletter— she hadn't kept a copy. The lone color photograph was one of her crossing the street in front of the Fourth Precinct office. It looked as though it had been taken from above by someone standing on the top floor of the Fourth Precinct parking garage. With the greenery and sunshine of a clear spring day in the background, she knew it had been taken within the past few weeks, maybe even the past few days.

They'd been looking for signs of tampering with breakers, fuses and wiring. They'd checked windows and doors throughout the ground and basement levels, looking for any building access that was broken or had *accidentally* been left unlocked. Except for the main door and the security gate to the parking garage—both of which required a passkey or typed-in code—everything at the Corsican seemed to be locked up just fine. So how had he gotten in here? Any sense of normalcy she might have felt, any sense of privacy or security, rotated on its axis. "I think I'm going to be sick."

"No, you're not. You're in control, remember?" John went to the window at the end of the passageway and reached up to inspect it. "It's sealed tight." He swung his beam into the rafters above them. "In fact, they could use a little ventilation down here. Looks like the main door is the only access. When was the last time you were here?"

She thought back to when she and Travis had brought down the boxes of winter coats and extra blankets. "When the weather started warming up. I brought those clothes down."

"So that's been a couple of months."

"About the same length of time Danny's been out of prison."

"And no one else noticed it?"

"Maybe it just happened."

He returned to her side to shine his light over the creepy homage. "Let's get out of here."

Maggie was stunned by the violation of it all. Not only

had Danny gone off the deep end with his obsession, but he'd also broken in and done it in her own personal space. "It's like a shrine." Her breath stalled in her chest. "Or a setup for a wake."

"It's a sick mind is what it is." John's fingers wrapped around hers to pry them off the chicken wire. "We need to report this. And I want to talk to Joe and the landlord about the security here. As far as I'm concerned, it sucks."

"Wait. Not yet." She liked the feel of her hand inside John's sure grip, so she held on. But she planted her feet and only let him pull her away from the front of the unit. She wasn't ready to leave this part of the basement just yet. "I don't know what Danny's game is, but I'm going to figure it out. Why did he do this? How did he do it?"

John relented on his efforts to get her out the door, but he pulled her around the corner into the main passageway that cut through the two rows of lockers, probably so she wouldn't have to see Danny's handiwork. "Okay, then, let's think about this. All the tenants have a key to the main door dead bolt, right?" Maggie nodded. "So who has a key to the locks in here?"

"Just me." She suddenly thought to pull the ring of keys out of her pocket and went back to her locker. "I mean, every tenant puts his or her own lock on their individual storage unit. But everyone in the building has a master key to get into the catacombs here."

Maggie tried her key in the padlock on her door. When she couldn't get the key to slide in, John took it from her hand and tried it himself. "It doesn't fit."

"This isn't my lock."

He dropped the keys into her palm, then snugged her hand inside his and pulled her back. "That thug probably cut yours off to get inside, then replaced it with his own lock."

Now she was ready to leave and call it in. "I think breaking and entering is enough to put Danny back in jail for a long time and keep him there. Especially because he committed the crime against his former victim."

Something long and skinny crunched beneath Maggie's shoe. She tilted her flashlight down to the floor and backed up. "Eeuw." A line of large black ants were streaming from beneath the storage locker across from hers and disappearing under the door frame of her locker. Although the ants had now changed their path to curve around the squished carnage of her shoe, they just kept coming. Hundreds of them. Thousands, even. "Look at all of them."

"Carpenter ants."

"Joe said Miss Applebaum found some in her apartment. He went in and sprayed them for her, I guess. They must have relocated down here."

"Which means they're probably throughout the building by now." John didn't sound any more pleased to see the tiny invasion than she was.

Swarms of anything had always been a bit of an ick factor for her, but as Maggie and John stepped over what had looked like another crack in the floor until their lights showed it to be a moving, living thing, she had another disturbing idea and stopped. "What would draw them all the way down here? You don't think there's something else in my locker, something…rotting? Dead?"

"Don't worry. They eat wood. Besides, we'd smell it if something was dead." He wrapped his fingers around her elbow and kept her from going back to see Danny's artwork again. Together they headed toward the garage. "These ants aren't as destructive as termites, but they're not good. Just one more reason to add to the list of why I never should have moved into this place."

Maggie tugged against his hand and glanced up at him. Was he already thinking about leaving?

With only the hint of a smile to warn her, he leaned in and planted a quick, firm kiss on her lips. "Don't worry, Sarge, you're on the list of reasons why I'm glad I did."

Maggie was smiling, too, by the time they left the storage space and reentered the parking garage. She liked seeing John smile. He was usually so serious and guarded. The flash of boyish teasing warmed her heart.

She'd liked the faintly possessive stamp of that kiss, too. Although she'd never imagined she would enjoy any man showing possessive tendencies around her again, there was something healthy and respectful, and completely new about the way John liked to hold her hands or take her arm, to subtly touch her—or kiss her. It was like falling in love for the first time all over again.

He made her feel important. He listened. He got angry... on her behalf. John made her feel like a woman worth caring about, not a punching bag or vessel for sex or thing a man owned the way Danny had. He made her believe that with the right man—with John himself, perhaps—that it was okay for her to love again.

She walked to her truck to pull out a spool of yellow crime-scene tape and marked off the entrance to The Corsican's storage locker, giving herself time to sort through those new feelings. She tried to decide if trusting John also meant she could trust herself enough to act on those feelings. But final decisions about her heart and trust and awakening desire would have to wait.

As soon as she was done securing the scene, she put in a call to dispatch. John was still poking around in walls and crevices while Maggie paced in front of the storage entrance's yellow tape and finished her call.

"I'd write up the report myself, but because it's my

stuff…I want everything to be by the book. Thanks. Hey, can you patch me through to Nick Fensom?" She covered the phone while she was being transferred to speak to John. "He's the detective who interviewed Danny. Nick booked him into a cell overnight, but if he's looking at Danny as the Rose Red suspect, then he'll want to see this."

"That's not the only crime in town, Sarge." John joined her next to the open doorway. "Even if he's not the rapist KCPD is looking for, he still needs to be put away for stalking you like this."

The dispatcher was on the line again. So much for an immediate response. "He's out? Could you just copy him on this report? And give him my number. Yeah, a unit to watch the place in the meantime would be great. Thanks."

Before she ended the call, John's cell phone rang. He pulled the phone from his belt and flipped it open to answer. "Hello?" He turned to face Maggie. "This is John."

His eyes locked onto hers, warning her that the call was important.

"Trav, where are you?"

Maggie darted to John's side. Fear made her blood run cold. This couldn't be happening again. "What's wrong?" She tugged on the sleeve of John's polo and stretched up on tiptoe to put her ear closer to the phone. "Why did he call you?" she whispered.

John put up a hand, asking her not to panic. "Yes, I know where your mom is." Then he twisted his wrist to check his watch. "Then you've got half an hour before practice is over. I'd be happy to come and get you, but I know she's planning on it."

Was her son in trouble again? Abandoned at the ballpark? Maggie grabbed John's phone and rocked back on her heels. "Travis, are you okay? Is somebody there with you?"

"Mom?" She knew that tone. She'd heard it before when she'd caught him bringing a garter snake into the apartment. When he'd painted his own set of roads on the carpet of his bedroom to run his cars and trucks. He was up to something he shouldn't be.

"Where are you?"

"At Abbott Field. I'm on the bench, waiting for my turn to bat."

"Coach Hernandez is with you?"

She hated the slight pause but appreciated the honest answer. "He's on the mound pitching. Hey, did you know I caught a fly ball today? Off Jimmy Stecher? He's our best hitter, but I got him out."

Great news, but missing the point. "Why would you think I wasn't picking you up today? Yesterday was just a fluke. I told you I talked to Chief Taylor and he said I could work my new schedule around yours."

"Well, I just thought...could we eat dinner with John again tonight?"

Huh? Maggie glanced up at John, who bent his head toward hers to catch more of the conversation. "Sweetie, we can't invite ourselves—"

"And maybe...you could wear a dress."

"A dress?" John's curious eyes narrowed on her.

"And some lipstick like the lady on TV."

"Why would I wear a dress for dinner? Did you tell John you couldn't reach me again? My phone is turned on—you didn't even try."

John's green-gold eyes swept down her dusty uniform and lingered on her legs. "*Do* you have a dress?"

Oh. Maggie's mouth dropped open. Heat crept up her neck and flooded her cheeks—partly from the hungry appreciation darkening John's eyes, and partly from learning that her ten-year-old was already wise enough in the ways of men and women to understand that showing a little skin—well, showing something a little more feminine than starched pants and a flak vest—could get a man's attention. And, apparently, he desperately wanted her to get John Murdock's attention. She snapped her mouth shut and turned away to focus on the call. "We don't even know if John has plans tonight."

"Ask him."

John's warm breath danced across the back of her neck. "If that's an invitation to dinner, I accept."

"Mom?"

Say it, Maggie. You know you want to. Do it. She glanced over her shoulder to the man standing behind her. "Would you like to come to dinner at our place tonight?"

Travis probably jumped off the dugout bench. "Yes!"

She turned her attention back to her son. "It's just a dinner invitation, young man. You have to go to bed early anyway. You were up too late last night."

"Mom, a guy has to eat."

"A guy has to eat."

The same phrase echoed in both ears at two different pitches. She might be in trouble. Not a bad kind of trouble, for a change, but a very unfamiliar kind.

She covered the phone and pulled it from her ear. "My son really likes you."

"That works out well because I really like him."

"He may not understand exactly what he's doing, but I think he's playing matchmaker with us."

An unexpectedly devilish grin teased the corners of John's mouth as he leaned in. "Good." His lips brushed across her nape, discovering a bundle of sensitive nerves and short-circuiting all thought and concern. "As slow as you and I are moving, somebody needs to."

"But—"

John circled his hands around the front of Maggie's waist and pulled her back against his chest so he could nuzzle his way along the side of her neck. Although she couldn't feel his body through her vest, she could definitely feel what his lips were doing above her collar. Her mouth opened in a noiseless gasp as a zillion little pinpricks of pleasure danced along her skin, chasing along the path where John's moist breath and patient, thorough lips heated her skin.

Who knew she had an erogenous zone right there? Who knew she even had an erogenous zone? Her pleasure had certainly never been the goal of Danny's sexual encounters.

"You like that?" John whispered against her ear.

She was barely aware of the "Mom? Mom?" in her ear.

But she wasn't so starved for male attention that she'd forget she had a young eavesdropper on the line. She tilted her head away from the sensual assault and tugged at John's arms, trying to work some space between them so she could talk to her son in a fairly normal tone. "Travis, I'm on my way to pick you up in just a couple of minutes. That's great about catching the fly ball. Be thinking about what you want to have for dinner. Love you."

"Bye, Mom."

When she handed the phone back to John, he used her outstretched hand to turn her. And then his mouth was back, sliding over hers. He slipped his palm beneath the collar of her uniform to cup and soothe the sensitized skin at her nape. But his fingertips were teasing wisps of hair free from the bun there. His tongue was in her mouth, exploring the soft skin inside.

Her tongue darted out to shyly play with his. Her hands were at his face, stroking the square line of his jaw, testing the rugged angles of his cheekbones, discovering the tantalizing contrasts of his warm scalp and short, spiky hair.

Heat blossomed inside Maggie, making her vision hazy, her hearing muffled. Her lips and tongue and fingertips seemed supernaturally aware of every taste—coffee and something tangy and sweet from lunch—and every touch—warm, sun-leathered skin, supple muscles moving underneath.

She felt her own body straining against the stiffness of her uniform, responding to John's embrace. She felt the greedy hand squeezing her bottom, the fingers loosening her hair.

She felt her holster butting against her hip, and the Kevlar solid as a wall between them. *Reality check.* She was a thirty-five-year-old woman of the world. She wore a gun and a badge. She had a son waiting for her at baseball practice. She had a job to do.

She wasn't the kind of woman who made out with a man in a parking garage. At least, she never had been.

"John, I'm on duty." Maggie leaned back, struggling to get some of the cool, dank air around them into her lungs to calm her senses. Yet she couldn't help wanting a taste of the salty skin along his jaw. Her brain cells were fighting to remember sanity and decorum, yet she ached at the subtle difference in textures on his skin as she pulled her fingers along the column of his neck, tracing healthy skin and scars down to the strong pulse beating at the base of his throat. "You're on duty, too, aren't you? We have responsibilities. You can't just kiss me like this."

"Then you need to stop kissing me back." His deep voice was a husky caress, a dare, a promise.

Maggie pressed her feverish lips against his. She kissed him again, more gently each time, lifting her hands to cradle his jaw and look up into his eyes. "What's going on with you? You seem…different."

John pulled back with a heavy sigh that stirred the tiny tendrils curling around her face. "You know, you're the second woman to say that to me today." He moved his wayward hands to a more neutral location at either side of her waist, and rested his forehead against hers, giving her some of the space she asked for without releasing her entirely. "Maybe I am a different man. It's like something finally woke up inside me today. Here I was, in a perpetual mood over never being able to go back to my old life. When I think, all along, I was meant to move on to something new."

"Me?"

"I don't know. But doesn't it feel right? I'm way out of practice, though—maybe I'm misreading the signs."

"You're not." Thank goodness he wore his hair like a marine, or her hands would have left it a rumpled mess. Still, she smoothed her fingers across his forehead as if there was a need to straighten the short spikes there. "Look, you can't be more out of practice at starting a relationship than I am. I really like you, John. I feel safe with you. But—"

"If you tell me you just want to be friends—"

"But I need to take it really slow. I've got a ten-year-old son. He idolizes you now, but I want you to get to know him. Some days he's an old man, trying to take care of me, and some days, he's still such a child. Plus, I've got a lot of emotional baggage that comes with me." She turned her head toward the disturbing shrine in her locker. "And I've got that kind of crap to deal with."

John slipped his finger beneath her chin and tipped her

face to his again. "I can do slow. If I can learn to walk again, I can learn to do relationships, too."

That probing gaze told her he could be interested in making something work with her. But too many years of guarding her body and her heart against another mistake was a difficult defense to get past. "I'm not easy to care about."

"I'll argue that one. I've got a need to take care of you in a way I haven't felt for any woman for a long time. I'm guessing it's harder for you to believe it than anyone else."

"Scary ex, remember?"

"One leg?" He tapped his thigh.

Maggie shook her head. "That doesn't matter to me."

"Well, I guess that one's hard for me to believe."

She curled her fingers beneath the collar of his shirt. "If I try not to do the crazy lady too often or too severely, will you try not to talk or think about yourself as though you're anything less than a good, wonderful man?"

With a reluctant nod that made her think he was as skeptical about making a relationship between them work as she was, he let go of her waist and pulled her right hand into his to seal the bargain. "Slow it is."

The sound of a man clearing his throat interrupted the intimate handshake.

Maggie quickly pulled away to see Joe Standage and his toolbox standing there with a wink-wink smile on his face. "Well, look at the two of you. Looks like romance is in the air."

Joe's teasing didn't bother her as much as seeing the man with the dark, round eyes and tan coveralls standing behind him. Lawrence Boyle simply nodded. "Mrs. Wheeler."

John's movements were as purposeful and methodical as Maggie's quick escape and throwing up of her invisible armor had been. He angled himself slightly between her and the other two men and slowly extended his hand to the man in the exterminator's uniform. "I don't believe we've had the pleasure. I'm John Murdock."

Boyle stared at John for a few uncomfortable seconds before shifting the canister he carried into one hand and shaking hands with the other. "Lawrence Boyle."

Although he seemed more at ease speaking to her than to John, the bleach-haired man didn't exactly look happy to see her. "Your friends at the police department are keeping him for a while. Left me shorthanded today. Now I'm working a double shift."

Was he expecting an apology?

John thumbed over his shoulder toward the storage lockers. "I'm guessing you're here for the ants."

"Yes, sir. Came back to have a look."

"Lawrence is my brother-in-law," Joe explained.

For some reason, Maggie had assumed Joe Standage was a perennial bachelor. "I didn't know you were married."

"My late wife—Lawrence's older sister—passed away several years ago. Long before I retired and took this job." Joe reached over and smacked Boyle's immovable shoulder. "I like to shoot some work his way whenever I can."

The first time Maggie had met Lawrence Boyle and his white van, a suspicion had planted itself in her mind, but she'd been too frantic about Travis's safety for it to fully register. It did now. She moved up beside John. "You said you were *back* to look at the ant problem. Have you been in the building before?"

"Have you been in the building in the past week?" John clarified.

Bug-eyed Boyle shook his head. "This was one of Danny's jobs."

"Danny was here?" She looked from Lawrence to Joe and back. She didn't care who talked, she just needed to know. "When?"

John stood right behind her. "Answer her."

"He sprayed some old lady's apartment upstairs—"

"That would be Miss Applebaum," Joe interjected.

"And laid down some foam around the foundation down here. About a week ago."

"The day I got that note and the elevator stopped."

Boyle's shoulders puffed up as if she'd accused him of something. "Once he told me you lived here, I made sure he came during the day while you were gone. I know your fifty-yard rule. He used to talk about you every day."

"In prison?"

"Yeah. We shared a cell for a few years. I know what you said he did to you."

"What he *did* do," Maggie emphasized. She'd lived it, and the court had proved that there'd been nothing consensual about the weekend Danny had captured her, brutalized her, dragged her back to their old apartment and kept her prisoner until he'd finally drunk enough to pass out and she could escape. "That's why he can never come near me or my son again."

Boyle shifted on his feet, looking either embarrassed by his past or uncomfortable about sharing too much about a man he considered a friend. "Ma'am, I need to get to work. Like I said, a double shift means it's a long day."

"Was Danny in the storage unit, too?" she asked.

"I don't know. That's why I'm here to check his work. See if he missed something, or sometimes it just takes a second application to kill the buggers." Boyle held up the flat-nosed nozzle and hose, and translucent plastic canister that contained a thick clear liquid and was marked *Poison*.

"They can chew a lot of holes in the wood and lay a lot of eggs if we don't catch 'em."

When he moved around her to enter the storage area, Maggie grabbed his arm to stop him. "I'm sorry, but you can't go in there right now. It's a crime scene. You'll have to do your work another time, or work in a different area."

"What happened?" He looked down at the hand on his canvas sleeve as if he wasn't any happier about her touching him than he'd been to take John's.

Maggie quickly snatched it away. "Someone broke into my storage locker."

"You think Danny messed with your stuff?"

"Someone did." John grasped her shoulders and pulled her a step back from both men. He made no effort to mask his suspicions that Joe and anyone he hired would have complete access to the building. "Someone who has a key."

Chapter Ten

Thirty-six hours without hearing from a violent ex might sound like a reprieve to some women, maybe even an end to their troubles. But Maggie knew that going a full day and night without hearing from Danny was more likely to mean he was plotting something even more cruel than anything he'd done to her yet.

Still, it was heartening to have made it through almost two normal days. She thought if she had enough practice at it, she could learn to do normal without second-guessing every move or comment she made.

Her dinner with John had been by turns fun and awkward. Even with Travis between them to keep the conversation going, it had felt like a first date. The sundress she'd worn had been a hit, judging by the appreciative peeks beneath the table from John. But then she'd spilled her iced tea down the front of it and been forced to change into jeans and a T-shirt—and it seemed the glances were just as heated. She'd been nervous each time one of them asked a question that was a little too personal and the other paused before answering. And then, after putting Travis to bed, she and John had curled up on the couch together to share some more adult conversation. But the two hours of sleep she'd gotten the night before caught up with her and she'd promptly fallen asleep.

She'd warned John that she'd be a slow mover in the relationship department. But it was embarrassing to think just how much patience it would require of a man who wanted to be with her. She had to question if a man like John—so wounded by life the way she had been, and still searching for his own emotional healing—would have the patience and endurance to put up with her bad days as well as her good ones.

Work had gone a little better. She'd been invited to sit in on two victim interviews, one with Dr. Kilpatrick and one with Detective Montgomery. In the first interview, Maggie's sharing of some of the emotions she'd carried with her since her own attack had encouraged one of the Rose Red Rapist's earliest victims to share about her abduction. She'd been a young woman in graduate school back then, and had gone on to become a pediatric nurse, wife and mother of three children. Although she had no description of her attacker, she remembered being forced to bathe afterward—an early effort by the rapist to create a sterile crime scene that would leave no trace.

She'd met with the second victim this morning, an attorney who was more than willing to talk, but whose memory of the event had been blocked out by either emotion or time. Along with Detective Montgomery, Maggie had asked a few pointed questions that had helped the woman recall some specific details that matched Bailey Austin's account—the scent of chemicals—cleansers, perhaps?—and the clear plastic beneath her as the rape occurred.

Maybe she wasn't as successful about nailing Danny for stalking her, but she was beginning to feel that she was worthy of Chief Taylor's belief in her—that she might just make a good detective, and that she was making a meaningful contribution to the task force's investigation.

This afternoon, she'd joined Detectives Montgomery

and Fensom at the Fairy Tale Bridal Shop to conduct a different sort of interview—this time with the closest thing they had to an eyewitness of the attack, shop owner Hope Lockhart.

Maggie hovered in the background while she observed the two seasoned detectives in action. Hope was about as keen on being grilled by the two detectives as an actual victim would be. A plump young woman with glasses and curly blond-brown hair, Hope Lockhart fit the stereotype of a plain Jane. But because redheaded Maggie was the last person to relegate anyone to stereotype status, she focused on the woman's beautiful fashion sense and on the amazing diversity and apparent success of her business.

The entire time that the detectives were questioning her about the night of Bailey Austin's attack, Hope dressed a mannequin in a silver-colored satin wedding suit and added it to a black-and-white storefront display touting sophisticated second weddings. Even with her business partner, and the building's owner, Brian Elliott, on hand to offer his support, Hope stayed busy. Either she was worried about impressing her partner, or she needed to stay busy to keep her nerves from overtaking her.

"I really don't see what I can tell you," she said, swapping out a jeweled barrette with a netted hat to place in the mannequin's hair. "Of course I want to help. I've worked with Bailey and her mother for several months, planning her wedding. I'd like to think of her as a friend." She glanced at Detective Montgomery before switching back to the barrette. "But I didn't see anything."

Brian Elliott stood up from his chair in one of the seating areas near the shop's dressing rooms. "Exactly. Montgomery, is it?"

"Yes, sir."

Mr. Elliott handed off a file he'd been reading to his

executive assistant, a dark-haired woman named Regina Hollister. He buttoned the jacket of his expensive suit and invited himself into the conversation. "Hope is the most honest woman I know. If she says she saw nothing that can help you, then she saw nothing. Now we were having a business meeting when you showed up that I'd like to finish so I can get back to my office."

Spencer Montgomery slipped his hands into the slacks pockets beneath his own suit jacket, completely unruffled by the other man's defense of Hope and superior attitude. "You're free to leave anytime you want, Mr. Elliott. Miss Lockhart was one of the last people to see Miss Austin before the attack. She may have noticed someone lurking in the area who shouldn't have been there—"

"I didn't."

"Or seen an unfamiliar vehicle." Maggie noticed the wheels turning behind Hope Lockhart's glasses, as though she was trying to place something she had seen that night. "And she would certainly be able to tell us Miss Austin's state of mind when she left the bridal shop."

"She was upset." Hope worked the small hat between her fingers as she faced Spencer. "Bailey and her mother were arguing about the wedding. She wanted this classic outdoor ceremony in the backyard of her father's estate. Small, with family and a few friends—something to do with wanting her sister to be her matron of honor. But her sister doesn't deal well with crowds of people."

Spencer's attention was focused solely on the shopkeeper now. "I've met her sister. That would fit."

Apparently giving up on moving the interview along, Brian Elliott returned to his seat. Nick Fensom, who'd been wandering through the salon, casually looking at the displays of clothes, invitations and gifts, ended his exploration near the same seating area. Maggie guessed he was positioning himself to run interference for his partner if Elliott decided to intercede again, so that Spencer could concentrate on Hope Lockhart's story.

Maggie was beginning to rethink the shy appellation she'd given Hope earlier. Although her nerves were about to crush the small hat, she seemed equally determined to offer useful information. "To be honest, I felt like Bailey's mother and her fiancé were ganging up on her. Mrs. Austin-Mayweather said she'd reserved a date at a cathedral and wanted Bailey to look at big ball gowns. And her fiancé—"

"Harper Pierce."

"Yes. Harper seemed just as eager to have a big wedding as his mother-in-law. He kept talking about social contacts and publicity and expectations of the family name."

"And Miss Austin didn't want any part of that?"

"My job is to listen to the bride—to help make *her* dream come true. I tried to stand up for her, but I'm not terribly persuasive." Perhaps seeing the damage she'd done to the hat, or just needing a break, she returned it to a box of tissue paper on the counter. "Bailey threatened to call off the whole wedding. They argued about it all the way out into the parking lot."

"Where our perp probably heard the commotion that drew his attention to Miss Austin."

Hope's posture visibly wilted before she faced Spencer Montgomery again. "I was locking up the shop and turning out the lights before going to my apartment upstairs when I saw her walking past the front window. I should have gone after her."

"Did you see any vehicles following her?"

Hope moved her head from side to side in disbelief. "Harper and Mrs. Austin-Mayweather pulled out of the parking lot and turned that direction. I thought they were going after her. Why wouldn't they give her a ride?"

"She probably refused if she was angry."

"I should have invited her back into the shop. I could have saved her."

Maggie stepped out of the background at the woman's growing distress. "Don't blame yourself. Once a guy like that sets his mind on a target, he won't stop until he gets what he wants. He saw someone who was vulnerable and alone, and he went after her. Chances are if you'd gone out there and gotten in his way, you might have become the victim instead."

"Me?"

"Now you're just scaring her." Brian Elliott was back on his feet. He slipped an arm around Hope's shoulders. His protective paternal look included Maggie as well as the detectives. "I think it's time for you to leave."

Spencer pointed to the small cameras placed inside both the front door and the side entrance to the parking lot. "I don't suppose you have security cameras installed *outside* your building and this shop where we might have captured a picture of the man following Miss Austin?"

Brian Elliott never took his eyes off the detective who'd challenged him. He merely tightened his arm around Hope's shoulders and pointed to his assistant. "Reggie, make a note to get exterior cameras installed tomorrow. I want Hope to feel safe here."

"Yes, sir."

Spencer Montgomery had heard enough. Reaching inside his jacket, he pulled out a business card and handed it to Hope. "Miss Lockhart, thank you for your time. If you think of anything else, or you see any other suspicious activity in the neighborhood, please give me a call."

She squeezed the card in her hand. "I will."

Nick was already opening the front door as Spencer acknowledged the others in the shop. "Mr. Elliott. Ma'am. Have a good meeting."

On her way out the door, Maggie's phone vibrated on her belt. When she saw Annie Hermann's number, she apologized for delaying the two detectives. "I need to take this. It's the crime lab—about that break-in I had at my place."

"Go ahead." Nick waited for a young professional couple bending over the same smartphone to pass by on the sidewalk before pulling back the front of his leather jacket and stretching his shoulders and neck. "I want to do some checking around the outside of this place, see what kind of vantage point our guy had to have if he spotted his vic in the parking lot."

Detective Montgomery was less affable. "Are you kidding me?" But Maggie saw that his irritation was directed at the dark-haired reporter lounging outside his SUV across the street. Gabriel Knight nodded to the two young women carrying their cups of coffee into the nearby office building before pulling off his sunglasses and turning toward the three of them. "What do you suppose he wants?"

"Besides the scoop on breaking our case?" Nick teased. "Or taking another potshot at us in the morning edition?"

Spencer waved Nick off before checking pedestrians and traffic and stepping into the street. "You two take care of your business. I want to make sure Knight doesn't hassle Miss Lockhart—or any other witnesses around here we need to talk to."

Hanging back on the sidewalk while the two men went to work, Maggie answered her phone. "Hey, Annie, sorry about that. We were finishing up at the bridal shop. Did you find anything on Danny?"

Annie's sigh gave Maggie the answer she didn't want to hear. "Sorry. The only prints we found in your storage locker were yours and Joe Standage's."

Maggie released a frustrated breath of her own. "Joe helped me move stuff down there this winter. What about outside the locker or on the news clippings themselves?"

"Nothing. I went over everything myself. Your guy was wearing gloves. Forensically, we can't prove it was Danny Wheeler who broke in there."

The man was smart, which only made him more dangerous. "Okay, thanks."

"No problem. Hey, we're on the same team, right? Anything I can help you with, you let me know."

"Same here. Thanks."

After putting away her phone, Maggie looked up and down the street, wondering how these busy blocks had looked at night to Bailey Austin, when the shops and offices had closed. It looked like a nice enough neighborhood on the surface—maybe not as cosmopolitan as it had been in its original heyday. But it was no longer the rundown, homeless crime lane it had once been either. Much of the historical architecture had been restored. There were new businesses going in, thriving shops, a café, apartment living on the upper floors.

Just how truly alone had Bailey Austin been that she jumped out as a target to the Rose Red Rapist? It was hard to picture it now, with the clear blue afternoon sunlight, and the bustle of activity on the streets and sidewalks.

Had someone been inside one of those doors or windows who might have seen something? A custodian cleaning an office perhaps? Or someone else who lived above his or her business like Hope Lockhart did? There were several night spots within a couple of blocks in either direction. Had there been no overflow parking on this street? No couple strolling hand in hand on a date?

What made Bailey Austin the rapist's target? There were so many women here who fit the same general description.

A camera flash of understanding went off in her head. Maggie's gaze shrank from the big picture she'd been contemplating down to the individual faces of each woman on the street.

"Nick?" She spun around, looking for the burly detective. "Nick!" She jogged down to the entrance to the Fairy Tale Bridal Shop parking lot to catch him before he disappeared around the corner. "I just realized something."

"What's that?"

She pointed to the people in their cars and walking past on the street. "Look at the women here. They're all professionals." Some were younger, perhaps newly out of college and chasing after a new career. Others were older, well-established by the look of their BMW or designer bags. They had different ethnicities and looks, but they were all a certain type. "Detective Montgomery talked about Rose Red having a hunting ground. All the victims have been career women. They've all had money and class, or were well on their way to having both."

Nick nodded, seeming to find merit in her assessment. "Women with self-confidence, authority. Women who are going places."

"Upset or not, he picked up Bailey Austin here because she was the right type of woman."

"And he knew he could find that type in this neighborhood."

A little rush of excitement buzzed through Maggie's blood. They were onto something here. At least they might be able to narrow down their search area for where the serial rapist might strike next. "That's why our guy has gone after blondes and brunettes and different racial types. It's not a look he's targeting, like most serial rapists. He has a thing for women who have power. Strong women. He didn't go after Bailey Austin because she was upset and vulnerable. He went after her because she was strong enough to stand up for herself against her fiancé and mother. In public."

"I'm telling Spence to get his butt back over here. You okay to get back to the station on your own? He can drive me in his car." She nodded as he pulled out his phone to text a message. After hitting Send he held out his arm to give her a congratulatory fist bump. "Good profiling, Wheeler. How come you never made detective before?"

"I didn't have the college degree."

"What took you so long to get it?"

She held up her wrist and pointed to the time. "Because I have a ten-year-old who's playing a baseball game in an hour. I've been kind of busy raising him."

"He any good?"

"He will be. Apparently he has a good eye for catching pop flies. Now if we can just get him to step into the pitch when he swings the bat."

"Sounds like my kind of evening." He groaned as if he knew he'd be spending his evening doing something much less enjoyable. "Get out of here and enjoy the game. I'll mention what you said to Spence."

"Thanks." She headed for her truck down the street.

"And Wheeler?"

"Yes?"

Nick Fensom grinned. "File the promotion paperwork. You'll make a damn fine detective."

A damn fine detective.

Nick's praise and her own sense of success buoyed her

spirits in a way she hadn't felt for weeks now. Her life wasn't perfect, but things were definitely heading in the right direction. Both personally and professionally, she'd made some choices that just might pay off if she kept working hard at them.

· She was waiting in traffic at the intersection where Bailey Austin had been attacked, looking forward to Travis's game and seeing John and getting a good report with Chief Taylor, when the light changed and her mood sank like a popped balloon.

Parked at the corner was a white van, with a bug and rat and Boyle's Extermination logo painted on the side. And behind the steering wheel sat Danny Wheeler.

Watching her.

JOHN PATTED TRAVIS'S left leg. "This one here." He covered the boy's hands with his own around the handle of the bat and swung it with him. "Go forward. Don't step out. You're losing the amount of space over the plate that your bat can cover, so you have less chance of hitting anything. And remember, keep your eye on the ball all the way to the bat, or to the catcher's mitt if you decide to take the pitch."

"Keep my eye on the ball. Right." Travis nodded. The boy stooped down to smear his hands in the dirt, spit on them and rub them together. He knocked twice on his helmet before gripping the bat and aligning his stance the way John had shown him. "Like this?"

John grinned at the theatrics as he stood back and watched Travis take a couple of swings on his own. It felt like forever since he'd been that young and eager to imitate the big leaguers he'd watched on TV and at Kaufmann Stadium. "With a little less fanfare that's it. You'll get more power moving into the ball like that, too."

"How's that swing coming?" John looked up to see the

copper-haired police officer walking toward them with a sports drink and bag of sunflower seeds in her hands.

"Hi, Mom." Travis ran over to the fence to pick up his game supplies and accept a casual, just-an-arm-around-the-shoulder hug from Maggie. "I'm gonna get a hit tonight. John showed me how."

"Fantastic."

A shout from Coach Hernandez summoned all the boys to end their warm-ups and join him in the dugout.

"Thanks, Mom!"

"Have a great game. Do your best." Maggie cheered him as he ran across the diamond.

John scooped up a couple of practice balls on his way to the fence. Now that Travis was gone and the field lights were coming on, a glance at Maggie's pale skin and the time on his watch made him suspicious of the smile on her face. "You're late. Everything okay?"

She followed him down to the gate on her side of the fence. "There are four games going on here tonight. I had to park clear at the far end of the lot and walk a quarter of a mile."

"Hey, Mom!" They both turned at Travis's shout. "Don't yell my name, okay?"

"Okay." Maggie flashed her son a thumbs-up. "Go get 'em." Her eyes were on the concrete path before them when he joined her at the base of the bleachers. "Thanks for getting him to the game."

"We got some practice in." She still hadn't made eye contact with him. Instead, she was eyeing the parents and grandparents in the stands, and looking beyond them to the people lined up at the concession stand and still milling in the parking lot. He had to concentrate for a moment on where he was placing his false foot as they climbed the open stands, but he didn't have a good feeling about this. "Sarge, what is it?"

She slid between two rows of metal seats and sat. "How about here? Are we too far up?"

Uh-uh, she wasn't getting off that easily. He sat down beside her. "I've had warmer greetings from enemy troops. What's wrong?"

He silently dared her to say *nothing* and take them several steps backward in this tentative relationship. But there was a reason he admired her courage. Her darting gaze finally landed on him. "I saw Danny this afternoon."

"But his restraining order—"

"He was far enough away that I couldn't cite him for anything. But he was close enough that he could watch me. We were out around the city, conducting interviews. I don't know how long he was following me." John's blood heated with protective anger and he, too, started scanning the perimeter of the ball fields and park, searching for the enemy. "I took the scenic route to get here, and lost him. But he already knows where Danny plays, so he could show up again."

"You want to go home?"

Her cheeks flooded with a healthier color. "I'm not taking Travis away from his game."

"Good. I'd rather see you ticked off than afraid. Danny Wheeler doesn't get to control your life. Not anymore." For John, it was a personal vow. That bastard was never going to hurt Maggie or rob her of that genuine smile again. Not on his watch. And he wasn't planning on going anywhere anytime soon. "Let's sit here and enjoy the game," he suggested. "And Danny can just hide in the dark and miss out on what really matters in life."

"Family and friends?"

John turned toward the field. "Baseball."

She laughed out loud, as he'd hoped. But she surprised him by capturing his jaw and pulling him closer to press a kiss against his cheek. "Thank you."

It was brave and spontaneous and perfect.

He smiled and leaned in farther to kiss her squarely on that beautiful mouth. "I like that even better than being ticked off."

Yeah, that was the smile he wanted to see. And he had no problem when Maggie laced her fingers together with his and leaned her shoulder against him. John held on tight, enjoying the game, Travis and the woman who was becoming more and more vital to him with every passing second.

He'd come a long way from that roadside bomb in Afghanistan. Maybe, just maybe, this was what finally coming home was supposed to feel like.

And no coward watching from the darkness was going to steal it away from him.

"THAT WAS MY FIRST DOUBLE."

John lined up the darkened park entrance in the beam of his headlights and turned into the empty parking lot as the victory celebration that had been going on since he offered to take Travis and Maggie out for ice cream after the game continued. "I think we've pretty much figured out that if we can get you on base, buddy, you're a fast runner. Is that the first time you've scored a run this year?"

"Yep." He heard a crunch from the backseat of his truck. "Dat's da foost time I 'tole a base, too."

Maggie turned in the passenger seat to lay down the mom law. "Not even ice cream stops your chatter. Now you finish that cone before it melts all over John's truck. Leaving a mess isn't a very nice way to thank him."

John wasn't worried. "It washes off."

She passed a paper napkin back to Travis and faced the

front again. "I'll have to wash him and his uniform off, too. Once the sugar and excitement wear off that boy's going to crash."

"It was a great night, wasn't it?" John reached across the seat to touch his fingers to Maggie's, sending the message that he was talking about more than just a baseball game.

She shifted her hand to link them together palm to palm, letting him know she got the subtle message, even though she answered, "That was the Tigers' first win of the season. Awesome job, Trav."

"Uh-hmm."

While Travis stuffed the last of his chocolate ice cream into his mouth to continue discussing his exploits, Maggie pointed to the dark pickup in the shadows at the far end of the lot. "That's me."

John slowed to pull up beside the truck. "If you want to leave him buckled up and his gear in the back, I can just follow you home." He turned on his brights to give her a clear, safe path to her driver's side door and stomped on the brakes. There was nothing *safe* about what he saw. "Sarge."

"Oh, my God." Maggie was out the door before John could stop her. "Stay back."

Like hell.

"Maggie!" He glanced into the rearview mirror. "Stay in the truck, buddy," John ordered. He killed the engine and climbed out, leaving the lights on to illuminate the atrocity parked before him. Grabbing Travis's baseball bat from the bed of the truck, he armed himself before hurrying after Maggie.

She flinched when he caught her by the arm to pull her back but refused to let her go.

"Do you think they can find some evidence now?" he

growled, wishing she'd let him turn her away from the vandalized truck.

There wasn't a window that hadn't been bashed in or splintered by dozens of hard blows. The headlights were toast, the hood and fenders dented in by something long and narrow—like the bat he held.

And that devastation wasn't the worst of it. The front tires had been punctured and all manner of vile things had been carved into the paint by a very angry hand. *Mine. Liar. Bitch.*

If he hadn't been so alarmed by the unblinking pallor of Maggie's expression, he would have heard the footsteps a moment sooner.

"Mom, what's a 'who-ree'?"

"Travis!" Responding like a fierce mama bear when she wouldn't protect herself, Maggie grabbed her son, hugging him tight to her chest and turning him from the graphic image of what Danny Wheeler had wanted to do to her. "Don't look, sweetie. It's not a nice word. None of it's nice. Don't look."

"Mom?"

"Let's get him out of here." John hated the tremor he heard in Travis's voice. He hated that either one of them had to ever see something like this. He wound his left arm around Maggie's waist, shielding both mother and child in his embrace. He moved them out of the light from his truck, making them harder targets to spot.

"Is this when we go to a safe place and call the police?" Travis asked.

"Yes." Maggie's voice was stronger now. She was moving with a purpose. "Yes, sweetie, that's exactly what we need to do right now."

John urged them both back to his truck, all the while scanning the ball diamonds and parking lot and street beyond for any sign of movement, any vehicle that didn't belong. He briefly wondered if it was worth leaving their side to break into the maintenance booth and turn on all the ballpark lights again. He opened the door and Maggie helped Travis scramble up into the backseat before climbing into the passenger seat and pulling out her phone. "Lock it. Call for backup. Get a BOLO out for Danny Wheeler."

Maggie nodded and punched in a number. He was going for the lights. But almost as soon as John turned away, the truck started behind him and he whirled around to see Maggie lowering the automatic window. "Where are you going?"

John spun the ball bat in his fist and peered into the darkness. Evil was lurking out there in the shadows. Of that, he had no doubt. "I'm gonna find that bastard, or at least some sign of where he went."

She unsnapped the holster on her belt and pulled out her GLOCK. She pushed it out the open window, butt first. "Then take this."

He pushed it right back. "No, you keep it. Wheeler's the kind of man who beats up women and empty trucks. He doesn't have the guts to come after me. If he shows his face before I get back, shoot him."

LIKE A COCKROACH CLINGING to the dark places of the world, Danny Wheeler had refused to show himself and face John's protective wrath. But he'd left a trail that even a private on his first sortie could follow.

With the park lights now casting daylight over the nearest ball field and parking lot, John knelt next to a pair of skid marks on the concrete pavement. The stripes of black rubber beneath the paint chips and shattered glass indicated a quick stop and speedy retreat.

The suited-up detective with the light red hair who'd introduced himself as Spencer Montgomery and taken charge of the scene nodded his agreement. "Something big stopped here."

Maggie followed right behind the detective. "Like a white van?"

"That'd be about the right dimension to match this wheel base." John pointed out the bits of displaced gravel around Maggie's truck. "And those are definitely man-sized footprints."

John braced his knee and pushed to his feet as Detective Montgomery nodded. "I've already put out an APB on the bug van and Wheeler. We'll find him, Maggie."

An outburst of laughter from the back of John's truck, where Montgomery's partner, Nick Fensom, was playing some kind of game with Travis to keep the boy's attention off the disturbing scene, turned Maggie's head. But only for a moment. John could tell that something had changed inside her, something had hardened knowing that Travis had seen this. Whatever bond of fear Danny held over her had finally been burned out by pure, white-hot anger. She wasn't the skittish, paranoid woman John had first met on the elevator that day. Knowing that her innocent son, who'd never known his father, had finally gotten a glimpse of the unspeakable things he'd done had finally enabled her to seize the courage and strength she possessed.

"Nick's good with kids." She pointed out the obvious.

"Probably because he's the oldest of six brothers and sisters."

Maggie still worried like a mom, but she was thinking like a cop now—not a battered spouse who lived in constant fear of her ex's return. She went to stand by John and face the detective. "How did Danny get out of jail so quickly?"

Montgomery shrugged his apology. "We tried to hold him, but his boss, Lawrence Boyle, posted bail. He's a free man until his assault hearing, unless we can pin this or something else on him. Then I doubt he'll ever be a free man again."

John wanted a better answer. "Can't you arrest him on suspicion or take him in for questioning and lose the key to his cell? Who else would do something like this to Maggie?"

"We have to find him first," the detective pointed out. "But we will. Doing something like this seems like suicide for a man who wants to stay out of prison. But because he's so keen on going back, I'm happy to put together a case and oblige him."

John liked the cool, methodical thoroughness he saw in Montgomery's documentation of the crime scene and questions he'd asked Maggie. If there was evidence to be found and a case to put together, this guy would get the job done.

He slipped his hand to the middle of Maggie's back. There was nothing more he could do here—Wheeler was smart enough to be long gone. "Is it okay if I take Maggie and Travis home? It's getting late and he's got school in the morning."

The detective nodded. "Sure. Let us work on this. I'll order an extra patrol unit to keep an eye on your building."

"Thank you." Maggie leaned back against John's hand, no doubt feeling the emotional fatigue of the day.

Montgomery may have noticed it, too, because he reached out to give Maggie's shoulder a supportive squeeze. "I need you to focus on the Rose Red case, and that talent you have for getting the victims and witnesses to open up and talk. You don't need to be dealing with this sick…" The tension in his voice faded away to silence. "I guess that's why you relate so well to the victims."

"Call me if you find out anything," Maggie said, turning toward her son.

"I'll see you at work tomorrow." John paused, a step behind her when Montgomery put up his hand. "Are you military?" he asked.

"United States Marine Corps, sir."

"Are you staying with her and the boy?"

Maggie came back, making a polite argument that John wouldn't hear. "John lives next door. I wouldn't ask—"

He'd answered the call of duty more than once in his life. He'd answer it again.

"Yes. They won't be alone."

Chapter Eleven

"We'd better put these away." Maggie slipped the navy blue Marine Corps jacket from beneath Travis's limp hand and tucked his arm beneath the blanket and sheet. She swept the shock of chestnut hair off his forehead and leaned over the bed to kiss his sweet, unfurled brow. "I don't want anything to get wrinkled or broken."

As stressed out by the clear threat against her as he'd been excited about the ball game, Travis had been too wired to sleep. But John had had the brainstorm of bringing over his uniform and medals and sidearm to reassure her son that he was someone who could keep him well and truly safe.

The gun had quickly been stored away alongside Maggie's, but the ploy worked. Soon enough, Travis's natural curiosity kicked in and he'd begun to ask questions. Maggie had sat on the bed beside Travis while John patiently answered each one, sharing the meaning of the USMC logo and the brass buttons. Why he had captain's bars and what a major, colonel and general's brass would look like.

And then he'd brought out his boxes of medals and Travis's face had lit up with real awe. Maggie listened, too, tearing up with heartbreaking sadness as John glossed over the more gruesome details of a routine patrol cut short by a roadside bomb, and the selfless sense of duty it took for a man with a shattered leg to crawl back and forth between a bunker and the burning vehicle to retrieve his wounded and deceased friends.

For once, Travis had been silent, hanging on to every word of John's story. "You never gave up, did you, John?"

"No, son. A marine never gives up."

Tears burned along Maggie's cheeks and dripped into her lap at John's matter-of-fact account of the tragedy that had earned him his Silver Star. And even though Travis might not have fully comprehended the magnitude of John's sacrifice, he understood enough to know that with this man, he would be cared for and safe.

"Oops." Just as Maggie reached for the felt box in Travis's other hand, he rolled over in his sleep, hugging John's Purple Heart medal as close to his chest as he'd held his ball glove the night before.

"Let him keep it." John picked up the other medals from the bedside table. "If it helps him sleep." He cupped his hand over the crown of Travis's hair. She could see the impulse to lean in before he stopped and asked, "Do you mind?"

Maggie smiled her permission. "He'd love it." She could easily understand how safe and assured Travis felt when the tall, muscular marine bent down and gave her sleeping son a gentle goodnight kiss, as well. "You're his hero. Mine, too."

"I was just doing my job."

She swiped the dampness from her cheeks at the humble comment and closed the door to Travis's bedroom before following John out to the living room.

"Don't tell me you're all heroed-out. The man I saw tonight—" she paused to turn on a lamp and summon the courage to say what was in her heart "—the man I've seen every day since I met you is a hero." She shook out the folds in his jacket and held it out for him to put on. "May I?" When he reached out to take it from her, she pulled back a step and tilted her face up to his. "Please? I'd love to see you in it. I have a feeling you're stunning in your dress blues."

"Stunning?"

Okay, maybe not the word a marine wanted to hear. But when she refused to let go, he relented and turned his back to her so she could help him slide his uniform jacket on over his T-shirt.

"There you go." He held his arms out to either side and turned. *"Semper Fi."*

When he faced her again, Maggie saw the man she knew him to be inside, the same man she wished he could see. She supposed she should come up with a different word to describe the man she was looking at right now—hot, impressive, noble, sexy, patriotic, proud, powerful, handsome.

"Well?" he prodded, waiting for her opinion.

"Stunning."

John grinned, shook his head and started to shrug out of the jacket.

"Wait." Maggie picked up the box with his Silver Star and opened it.

"Sarge…"

"It's not complete yet." She pulled out the prestigious medal and unhooked the clasp.

His hands settled at either side of her waist and he tried to look stern with her. "Maggie…"

"Shh. Let me."

He touched his fingertip to the corner of her eye and traced the salty track of a tear down her cheek. "Will it make these go away?"

She nodded.

"Then do it."

Humbled and honored by the permission bestowed on her, Maggie slipped her fingers inside the front of his uniform to protect his heart as she pinned the medal above the pocket. She felt his chest heave against the back of her hand as some deeply hidden emotion surfaced. His fingers slid beneath her blouse and massaged the skin above the waistband of her jeans, as though holding still for her was almost more than he could endure. She pulled the pin back through the material and sealed the clasp. John leaned in to rest his forehead against hers.

Maggie outlined the ribbon with her finger and touched each shiny point of the star. Then she rested her hand over the medal, over his heart, and smiled. She tilted her eyes to look up into the unblinking intensity of his. "Your character, your commitment, your caring—those are the things that make you a hero, John. Not this medal." She slid her hands higher, framing the stubbled warmth of his jaw between them. "But maybe every now and then, if you look at this or your Purple Heart, you'll remember the men whose lives you saved. And the ones who helped save yours." She stroked her thumb across his lips and felt him shudder beneath her touch. "And maybe you'll remember what makes you a hero to my son. And to me."

She stretched up on tiptoe to replace her thumb with her mouth. She kissed him gently, felt his hands nip into her waist. She kissed him again, more firmly this time, and his lips chased after hers when she pulled away. Green-gold eyes locked onto hers. And then John's arms snaked behind her back, drawing her tight against his chest and lifting her so he could claim her mouth in a fierce, passionate kiss.

Maggie wound her arms around his neck and held on as

the emotions she'd unleashed poured out of him with every kiss and caress. She met each foray—taste for taste, touch for touch, need for need. He squeezed her almost painfully tight, imprinting brass buttons against her breast and stomach. His hands slid inside her blouse, dipped inside her jeans, stroking her skin, sending shivers along her spine even as she grew feverishly hot.

"John," she whispered, brushing her lips across his cheekbone, nibbling at his jaw. As much as she loved seeing him in uniform, she was beginning to think he needed to take it off. She wanted to touch the heat of his skin. She wanted to learn the supple movements of his body beneath her hands. She wanted to feel his thudding heart beating against hers.

His mouth opened warm and hot over the bundle of nerves beneath her ear and she gasped at the instant response in the tips of her breasts and deeper inside. With blind impatience, she pushed at the collar of his jacket and he quickly shrugged out of it and tossed it onto the couch. His lips moved from her throat down into the V of her blouse. He slipped one button free and rasped his tongue against the open spot.

"Your skin is so soft."

Another button opened and he dipped his tongue into the cleavage between her breasts.

"So pretty, so hot."

Her blouse fell open to her waist and John fit his big hands to her breasts, gently kneading, squeezing. His thumbs teased the proud tips straining against the confinements of satin and lace.

Each touch was a torment, every kiss a call that beckoned her to answer. She ached to feel his skin on hers, to feel his hardness against her curves. She wanted to feel the weight of him on top of her, inside her. It had been so long since she'd wanted. And she'd never wanted like this.

She tugged at the hem of his shirt and pushed it up beneath his arms to take the same liberties he had. She touched. His smooth muscles quivered beneath her hands. She closed her lips around his flat nipple and coaxed it to attention, tasting the musky flavor of his skin.

He groaned in response and slipped his hands down to cup her bottom and drag her up against the hard evidence of his desire. "Maggie, I want… I need… Can you? Will you?"

"Yes." Her answer was too breathy, too unsure. *Say it louder.* "Yes," she repeated. *Make this right, Maggie. Do it.* She pulled his mouth back up to hers and whispered against his lips. "Yes."

Seconds later, they were in her bedroom with the door closed behind them, tumbling onto the bed. Her blouse was gone, her jeans MIA. Maggie reached for the snap of his jeans and eased the zipper over his erection. But she got no further before his hands closed over hers and pulled them away. "Wait a second. Slow down."

"I don't need slow right now, John. I just need…" Oh, no. Had she done something wrong? Been too bold? Danny had never even asked her what she wanted, much less encouraged her to take the lead. Scrambling up onto her knees beside him, she grabbed a pillow from the headboard and hugged it over her chest, feeling suddenly unsure. "I'm sorry. What should I—"

John sat up and pressed a finger to her tender lips, silencing her. "Whatever you're thinking right now, stop it. And you don't need this." He plucked the pillow from her grasp and tossed it to the floor. "I want to see every beautiful inch of you."

Maggie followed him to the edge of the bed where he swung his legs over the side. "Then what's wrong?"

"There's not a damn thing wrong with you—with this." He combed his fingers through the loose waves of her hair and draped the ends over the swell of her breast, stroking her with the backs of his knuckles and raising chill bumps there. "I know my timing sucks, but…" He released her hair and raised his hips off the bed to tug his jeans down to his knees. "I need to take my leg off. It'll get tangled in the covers or it might knock against your shins or hit the bedpost if I'm not thinking about what I'm doing with it, and I don't want to bruise you or spoil the moment."

The self-conscious cloud cleared and Maggie knelt on the floor in front of him to help him pull off his shoes and jeans. When he was naked and vulnerable in front of her— his desire for her as obvious as the worry shining from his eyes—she bent forward to press a kiss to the elastic brace encircling his knee. She gently touched the strong, surprisingly lightweight post that extended down to his false foot. Tears scratched beneath her eyelids. "Oh, John. How you must have hurt."

"Actually, the burns killed most of my nerve endings." A tear spilled over at the suffering he'd endured. He cupped her cheek and brushed away the tear. "Hey, I thought these were going away."

If he could come to terms with his past and focus on this moment together, then so could she. With a brave smile, she sniffed away her sorrow and began peeling back the elastic band that covered the joint between his real and artificial leg. "Show me how."

"Ah, Sarge." She'd exposed the joint itself, revealing the miraculous testament to medical genius and the human will. "You don't have to do this."

"I want to." With gentle, reverent touches—and fingers

that were more sure than she'd expected—she followed his instructions and removed the prosthetic. She pushed his hand aside and took over the job herself when he massaged the rounded stump. "I'm not scared of this, John. It's a badge of honor, even more than your medals. I'm scared of…"

"Of what?" He pulled her up and fell back across the bed with her. He propped himself up on his elbow beside her and flattened his palm at the center of her stomach. "Maggie, what scares you?"

She was obliquely aware of the shorter leg falling on top of hers. Yet it wasn't the handicap she noticed, but the erotic differences between his crisp, masculine hair and her smoothly shaven thigh. She was aware of the corded strength in his leg, the arousal nudging against her hip. She was aware of the desire shading his hazel eyes and knew he was a powerful, potent man.

Maggie splayed her fingers over John's and looked down at them, embarrassed to speak the truth. "I haven't had sex in ten years, and I was never great at it, even before the rape."

For several awkward moments, John said nothing. And then he pulled his hand from beneath hers. "I'm not having sex with you, Maggie Wheeler."

Shocked at how easily he'd changed his mind, her eyes darted up to his. Embarrassed, heartsick, she tried to scoot away. "You don't have to do me any favors. If you think you're being noble or you're worried I'll freak out or—"

John rolled his body half on top of her, caught her chin in his hand and silenced her protest with a kiss. She went completely still except for the rapid rise and fall of her chest beneath his, and the needy, inevitable response his lips triggered in hers.

He finally pulled back when she was clutching at his

shoulders and shamelessly giving whatever he asked for in that kiss. She lay back on the bed, trapped in his eyes and confused by the delicious promise of his embrace. "I don't understand."

"I don't know what kind of garbage Danny put into your head, but we're not having sex." He pushed a bra strap off one shoulder and then the other. "I'm making love to you. Slow, wonderful, make-you-cry-out-my-name love to you."

The vow in those words made her blush. She felt the heat of them sinking into her blood and shimmering throughout her body. John dipped his head to kiss the rosy stain of heat on her breast. He kissed her again, pulling away the satin covering and tonguing the puckered nub of the nipple that sprang forth to meet him. Beneath his tender, thorough seduction, she moaned with helpless need. "Neither one of us is perfect. But together, I think we just might be."

It was an intoxicating promise. Maggie framed his face between her hands, drew his mouth back to hers and nodded.

"Yes, what?" he whispered against her swollen, tender lips.

"You're a good talker, John Murdock. Now show me perfect."

Soon, she was just as naked, just as needy, just as sure that being with John was what they both wanted. With her body on fire in ways it had never been before, she willingly climbed into John's lap as he sat up and pulled her onto his thighs. He entered her in a slow, patient stroke that finally bound them together as one. There was no need for words as they fell into a rhythm that took him deeper, faster, completely inside her.

She wanted to feel, to fly, to know the joy of loving a man who wouldn't hurt, who wouldn't take, who wouldn't force. She wanted to be with John Murdock tonight as much as she'd ever wanted anything in her life. He held her close, chest to chest, as the tiny tremors inside her quaked and grew.

And when he thrust up inside her, groaning with his release, and waves of sensation cascaded down all around him, Maggie buried her face in his neck because she did, indeed, cry out John's name.

LATER IN THE NIGHT, John awoke to the clinging blanket of the sleeping woman wrapped in his arms. Maggie's freckled skin was somehow both pale and warm in the dusky moonlight filtering through the blinds at her window. For all her height and strength and courage, she seemed fragile and vulnerable and oh, so feminine draped against his side, her bare breasts pillowed against him, the even rhythm of her breathing fluttering across his skin.

Humbled by the gifts of her passion and trust, he pressed a kiss to the soft jut of her shoulder. Then he extricated himself from her bed as gently as he could and pulled the covers up over her.

Dressing in nothing but his boxer shorts, he made a quick trip to the john to freshen up. Hopping on one leg, bracing his hand against a wall or door frame when he needed some balance, he made his way throughout the apartment, double-checking the locks on the front door, securing each window and making sure the answering machine was clear of any vile messages from Danny before he went into Travis's room.

The ten-year-old was sprawled out in sleep, covers kicked to the floor. John removed the medal box and set it on the lamp table beside the boy's ball glove before tucking the covers around him again and heading back to Maggie's bedroom.

"Is everything okay?" she asked in a warm, drowsy voice that made him want her all over again.

"We're safe. Travis is asleep and the placed is locked up tight. Everything's perfect." He climbed beneath the covers with her and gathered her into his arms. She might have been asking about her son or building security, but he was talking about her, this—Travis, too—all of it.

"John?"

"Yeah, Sarge?"

She walked her fingers across his chest and rose up in the bed beside him. "Is Travis hard asleep?"

"I think so."

"Then can we… Again?"

The covers had fallen to her waist and his thoughts zeroed in on her peachy breasts and how the cool, air-conditioned air excited them. His body responded with an instant heat at her shy request. "Oh, yeah."

He raised his head to capture a tempting breast in his mouth. She was so responsive, so giving, so beautiful. Without any words about hang-ups or handicaps, he pulled her down and rolled her beneath him, taking his sweet time to reacquaint himself with her body. He let her explore his as well until he was too hard and too needy to resist her mewling cries of pleasure any longer. She wound those long legs around his hips and welcomed him deep inside her feminine heat.

And when they were both sated and spent, he spooned himself behind her and they drifted off to sleep. Once upon a time, he'd gone to war because he couldn't forget a woman he could never have. Now his heart was so full of Maggie Wheeler and how much he loved her that he couldn't even remember any other woman's name. And he wasn't going anywhere.

John brushed her hair away from her face and kissed

the back of her neck. He nuzzled his nose in the scent of her there, finally understanding that of all the things he'd lost in his life, nothing could destroy him like losing this woman could.

"ARE YOU OKAY?"

Maggie smiled into her phone, wondering if she'd ever get used to having a man like John be interested in her welfare. "I'm fine. Really." She turned and waved to the uniformed officer who'd driven her straight to The Corsican's front doors after her shift at KCPD and a trip to the grocery store. "I'm home now. Someone was with me all day today and I'm about to knock on Joe's door to let him know I'm here."

Following their agreed-upon checklist of safety precautions, Maggie had called to report her location.

"I still wish you would have let me pick you up," John groused.

Maggie walked up to the building supervisor's door. She couldn't really do anything more unless she set down her bags of groceries or ended the call. "Your shift doesn't end until four, and because you're picking up Travis at school, it doesn't make sense for you to leave the station to bring me home, then go all the way back to his school and here again."

"I'd do it."

"I know you would, John." And even though she loved how he wanted to protect her, as a cop, she knew a thing or two about the protection business herself. Besides, "Knowing that you'll be there to get Travis home is a huge relief for me. I can watch out for myself. But when I'm worried about his safety, I tend to get distracted."

"Don't be distracted. Travis will be safe with me," he reassured her.

"I know."

"You call again as soon as you're in the apartment. And lock everything behind you," he reminded her unnecessarily.

"I will. I'll see you for dinner, then?"

"Sarge?"

"Yes?" She waited expectantly for him to continue. She knew they'd promised to move their relationship along slowly. But at what point did a man and woman declare their love for each other? When was it so soon that she'd scare him away? When was it too long that he'd lose interest in her?

And did she really need to hear the words from John? Danny had always been quick to tell her he loved her, even after the rape. From him, the words had meant nothing. From John, could she trust that they meant more?

But John said nothing further beyond, "I'll be there. Nobody goes in that apartment except Travis and me. Understood?"

Her disappointment rushed out in a soft sigh. She still had a lot to learn about a healthy relationship apparently. "Understood."

Once Maggie had ended the call and clipped her cell phone back on her uniform belt, she knocked on Joe Standage's door. The super had agreed to "clock her in" whenever she entered the building. But there was no answer at his door. Maggie knocked again and leaned her ear closer to his apartment door. There was no indication of movement inside. Had Joe been called to an emergency elsewhere in the building? Or was he not even going to get the simple request of being there to say hello right?

By the third knock with no answer, Maggie had already decided to head up to her own apartment. If she waited any longer than five or six minutes—ten minutes, tops—

to check in with John again, she had a feeling he would be calling her. Or even more worrisomely, skipping his promise to pick up Travis and heading straight here to make sure she was okay. So she punched the elevator call button and dialed Mr. Standage on his cell.

It went straight to voice mail. For a brief moment, Maggie considered trying his door again. But she hadn't heard another phone ring. If he was in there asleep or in trouble, surely she would have heard the ring. "Hey, Joe. Maggie Wheeler here. I just knocked on your door to let you know I'm home. Why don't you call me back when you get this message. Thanks."

The elevator dinged and the doors opened. She peeked inside to make sure it was empty, then swallowed her fear and stepped across the threshold. She clipped the phone back to her belt and punched in number 7.

Her breath caught in her chest as the doors slid shut and the car jerked, before beginning its slow rise up the shaft. *I should have taken the stairs.* But the groceries were heavy, she was a grown woman wearing Kevlar and carrying a gun, and John really would worry if she didn't call him soon.

When the elevator jerked a second time, Maggie gasped and grabbed on to the railing. Apartment, house, RV or tent—whatever her next home might be—she vowed that it would be located on the ground floor.

The 5 lit up over the doors and the elevator slowed its ascent. A scuffling sound on the outside of the car above her startled her. She glanced up at the fluorescent lights and decorative plastic grate on the ceiling. She trusted her eyes and willed her apprehension to dissipate. The light for the sixth floor lit up and she heard a thump. She glanced up again, a riot of goose bumps pricking across her arms and neck. Something was malfunctioning in the pulleys and machinery above her.

"Oh, God."

Some*one* was up there. The nightmare was happening again.

Maggie dropped her bags before the elevator jerked to an unnatural stop. She unholstered her gun before the service door opened. She flattened her back against the wall before the lights shattered and the ceiling crashed in and Danny Wheeler jumped down into the elevator with her.

"Hello, Mags." She raised her gun and he grinned. "At last we're together."

Chapter Twelve

Shock or terror or the adrenaline roaring through her blood created a moment's hesitation, giving Danny a split second of time to slam his arm down over her wrists as she pulled the trigger. The shot deflected off the ancient carpet and sparked against the steel wall. In the same follow-through of his swing he clamped his hand around her throat and pinned her against the railing.

Maggie kicked at his shins, shoved at his throat.

He snagged her wrist as she brought the gun to bear again and he slammed it into the wall beside her. One smack stung her knuckles. With a second blow her fingers went numb. With the third her grip popped open and the gun crashed to the floor.

Danny kicked it away before she could even gurgle a cry through the choke hold on her throat.

"Danny," she growled, "you're going to prison."

"I don't care." Picking her up by her throat and wrist, he hurled her across the elevator.

That was his first mistake.

She was closer to the gun now. Maggie pushed forward with her knees, stretched, reached.

"I saw you kiss another man." He kicked the gun away. He whirled around and kicked out again, his foot catching her in the abdomen below her vest and robbing her of breath. "You kissed him!"

Curling up into a protective ball, Maggie fought off the bruising pain and the flashback to another time and another blow.

"You were with him last night, weren't you?" He made the healing beauty of her time with John sound like a damning curse.

Truth or lie, there was no need for her to answer. He wouldn't listen.

"You promised to love me forever." Danny picked up her gun and pressed it against her belly. Maggie held herself still against the bruising poke of the barrel as Danny grabbed her phone and handcuffs off her belt. She inhaled a deep breath when he pulled away, then bit down on a fearful curse as he slipped the cuffs and gun into the pockets of his sweaty, grimy coveralls. Wherever he'd been hiding for the past twenty-four hours, soap and clean water hadn't been a part of it. "And now you're bangin' some other man?"

"Danny, don't." That one plea sneaked out as she watched him drop her cell phone into the empty hole where the elevator's emergency phone was supposed to be.

He reached up behind the panel and did something to the wires. The lights of the panel blinked on again. The machinery above her hummed to life as he pulled out his arm and straightened. He punched the *G* for the parking garage and the elevator began to descend. Maggie's heart sank with it.

"I made that same promise. I love you. I have always loved you. I always will."

His promise had ceased to have meaning long ago. "You have to let me go, Danny," she wheezed through the pain in her gut. "This is kidnapping."

He smoothed his fingers over his bald head, his hand coming away from his skin in a fist. She made the mistake of watching the fist when she should have been watching the boot.

"Shut up!" She rolled up at the last minute, deflecting his kick to a glancing blow off her vest. He kicked her again. "Nobody…" And again. "Tells me…" And again. She was saving herself from broken ribs, but the blows were robbing her of breath. "What to do! You're mine, understand? He can't have you!"

No, she argued with herself. *You're a different woman— stronger, braver.* She was smarter now than she'd been ten years ago. She had a son to live for, fight for. She had John Murdock in her life. She had hope for something better. Maggie knew how to fight back now. She wanted to fight back. She had to fight back. *Do it!*

With a primal scream, Maggie kicked out with her own feet, catching Danny's leg on the next blow and knocking him flat on his back. And then she was up on her knees, attacking him for all she was worth. She put her fists together and hit him square in the gut, stopping his cursing by stealing *his* breath.

She pushed to her feet, staggered to the control panel and pushed every button, ensuring a quicker stop. She sensed Danny rising behind her, smelled him closing in and rammed straight back with her elbow. His grunt of pain told her she may have cracked an unguarded rib. When he lunged for her again, she kicked straight for the groin and doubled him over.

"Help me!" She turned and pounded on the door. "Joe! Anybody! Call 9-1-1! Help!"

She had to get her gun. She had to stop the damn elevator.

"Why aren't we stopping?" she shouted.

"Because I'm smarter than you, bitch."

Too late, she felt the hand in her hair. She whirled around, kicked, punched. But Danny had her now. He slammed her head down against the railing and pain splintered through her skull.

Maggie dropped to her knees as the design in the carpet swirled into a blur and she felt like she might throw up.

She was going to die. She had a son to raise, a job to do and a man to love. And she was going to die.

She heard the click of the handcuffs and felt the pinch at her wrists. And then Danny was hauling her to her feet, capturing her, limp and woozy, against his side.

"I rigged the elevator, Mags. Just like I've rigged it before." He sounded triumphant as the *G* lit up and the elevator slowed to a stop. Blood was warm and sticky where it dripped into one eye, half-blinding her to the gun he pulled from his pocket. "You may be too stupid to learn that. But know this." He pressed a kiss to her temple and she nearly retched. "We love each other, Mags. And you will never be with any man but me."

Maggie heard a ringing in her head. It sounded like her phone, only there was no phone to answer. *Think, Maggie.* But the ache in her head was throbbing so badly that she could barely stand, much less keep a coherent thought in her brain.

When the doors opened, the instinct to run tried to clear her foggy senses, but her feet were like lead. Danny's arm anchored at her waist was the only thing that moved her forward, and when he stopped abruptly, she would have pitched to the concrete floor if he hadn't pinned her to him.

"Boyle, what the hell are you doing here?" Danny's seething anger prompted Maggie to lift her bound wrists to try to wipe her vision clear.

She blinked Lawrence Boyle's bleached-blond hair into

focus. "You said you were going to hide out at the shop," Lawrence explained calmly. "But you left. I knew you were coming to see Maggie."

Danny waved the gun at his friend. "Are you trying to get me arrested? Get that thing out of here." He pulled Maggie forward as he pointed to the extermination company's white van. "That thing's like a beacon for everyone in KCPD who's looking for me. What the hell were you thinking?"

Instead of replying to that, Boyle planted himself in their path, forcing Danny to stop. The bruises might not show up for a few hours yet, but there was no mistaking the blood on Maggie's face. "Did you hurt her?"

Maggie held out her hands, beseeching her only ally. "Help me. Please."

The dark bug eyes darted over to her. Boyle didn't look away until Danny spoke again.

"She's my wife. How I straighten her out is my business." Danny pointed the gun toward the van. "Now if you really want to help an old friend, you'll drive that thing away from here and take the heat off me."

"I'll help. Come with me."

As her deflated hope struggled to think of a way to outsmart two abductors instead of one, Danny dragged her to the back of the open van with Boyle. The burning stench of open chemical containers stung her sinuses and cleared her head like a whiff of smelling salts.

"What are you doin' with all this stuff, man?" Danny was as dumbfounded by the mess as she.

But Danny was only confused. She was instantly on alert.

The containers were empty.

"Oh, my God." She exhaled her fear on a soft breath, then ducked as Lawrence Boyle grabbed a wrench from the back of his van and swung it at Danny's head. The blow knocked him to the ground. Maggie staggered after the gun that slid beneath the van's rear tire, but Boyle beat her to it.

Before she could utter a warning, he pointed the gun at Danny's head and fired.

Maggie jumped at the sharp report that echoed throughout the garage. She tore her shocked gaze away from the pool of blood forming beneath Danny's head and looked up into the cool, emotionless expression on Lawrence Boyle's round face.

"Give me my gun, Lawrence," Maggie ordered, knowing her world had just taken a wild turn into Crazy Land. The relief she might have felt at Danny finally being purged from her life never came. This was something new to fear, something far less predictable than a violent ex. "Give me my gun."

Boyle looked at the handcuffs on her outstretched wrists, but made no comment or move to free her. He looked up into her eyes and smiled. "I took care of the problem for you, Maggie. Danny will never hurt you again."

"Thank you, Lawrence." Did she move in closer to try to reach the gun? Or should she retreat? Maybe it was enough just to keep him talking. "When the police come, I'll explain what happened. It was clearly self-defense. You were assisting an officer."

"I did that for you, Maggie. Danny was a bad man. I came to save you."

Maggie nodded. She tried to keep her focus on Boyle while scanning the garage for any sign of movement or sound. Two gunshots had been fired in the past ten minutes. The elevator had stopped and reversed course. A man was dead on the garage floor and no one was responding?

Her phone rang from inside the elevator again. John!

Please let one person notice that things were not right in her world.

Frustration screamed inside Maggie's head but she kept her voice calm. "Do you have a phone, Lawrence? We need to find my phone and call 9-1-1." She needed to get him to talk, like when she interviewed a victim or witness. It might mean the difference between living and dying today. "I'm worried about the chemicals you may have spilled." She glanced into the back of his van. "Where are all the poisons you killed the ants with?"

"You need to come with me." Maggie wondered if she was the one who was mad when he closed his beefy paw around one of her bound hands and led her toward the door to the storage lockers. "I wasn't sure how I was going to make this happen until Danny tried to take you away from me today. When he left the shop with his tools, I knew he was going to hurt you. I had to be here to stop him. He can't take you from me."

"Lawrence, no." *Please, no.*

He opened the door and led her inside. Once she crossed the threshold, the stink of chemicals—formaldehyde, permethrin, who knew what else?—was so heavy in the air that her eyes watered and she felt woozy again.

The door closed behind her, trapping her in the close space with only a sealed window at the end of the walkway. "What are you doing, Lawrence? How are you helping me?"

He stopped in front of her storage locker. The crime lab had taken all the newspaper clippings and left a black dusty mess of fingerprint powder over most of her things. Boyle pulled a ring of keys from his pocket and reached for the padlock on her door.

The lab had taken Danny's lock and replaced it with a

new one, but Lawrence jabbed his key at the lock as though he expected it to open.

Not Danny's lock.

The shrine, the pictures of her life, the clippings taped to the wall—they hadn't come from Danny. Danny hadn't gone through her things.

Maggie backed silently toward the door while Lawrence tried another key on his ring. The chemicals in the air, soaked into the wood and belongings all around her, were getting dense enough, toxic enough to make the open gash in her hairline burn.

When the keys didn't work, another man might have cursed. But Lawrence, with the strength of an ox and a chilly lack of outward feeling, leaned his shoulder into the wooden frame and barreled into it.

While wood splintered and chicken wire was pulled from the staples that held it in place, Maggie lengthened her silent steps toward the exit. The door was in reach now. She could turn, twist the knob...

"Don't leave me." She heard a small snap of sound behind her.

Maggie's blood froze in her veins. She slowly faced Lawrence again, expecting to see the gun pointed at her face.

Instead, he held a burning cigarette lighter.

"Don't do this, Lawrence." If he dropped that lighter... "You don't want to hurt me. Danny wanted to hurt me." She wondered how thick the fumes had to be before the air itself caught fire. "He ruined my truck and said terrible things to me. But you wouldn't do that." She gestured over her shoulder toward the garage. "You just saved my life. Danny wanted to kill me. But you saved me. You have to save me again."

"I love you, Maggie." His bulgy round eyes glistened

with tears. From the volatile chemicals? Or from the emotion that cracked his voice? "Not the way Danny did. My
love is pure and true. My feelings for you have sustained
me for a long time now. I've loved you from the moment
Danny first mentioned you."

"In prison?" *Get him to talk. Distract him. Stop him.*
"Did Danny talk about me when you shared a cell with
him?"

"Every night. Your picture was so pretty." He glanced
toward the empty wall of the storage locker. "I have more
pictures of you in here. I come here to look at you, where
I can be closer to you."

"You saved all those pictures of me?"

The lighter snuffed out, but he clicked it on again. "You
look so strong, but Danny said you needed to be taken care
of. I'm good at taking care of people."

"Yes, you are." She forced herself to focus on his eyes
and not the flame. "A lot of people are going to die if you
set this room on fire, Lawrence. The whole building will
burn. Help me again. Please. Let me go warn the people
upstairs."

He climbed over the broken frame of her locker and
pulled out her winter coat. He hugged it to his nose and
sniffed deeply, smiling as he pulled it away.

Maggie watched in horror as he held the lighter to the
hem of the coat and it burst into flame. "Boyle!"

It was unnatural the way it caught fire so quickly. He'd
doused it in the chemicals from his van. How many other
things in here would turn to ash that quickly? Or would
they simply run out of oxygen first?

"I tried to take care of you in little ways," he murmured
as he watched the coat burn. Maggie glanced up to spot the
sprinklers on the ceiling, then wrily despaired that they
were probably broken and that Joe Standage hadn't gotten

them fixed yet either. "I sent you your favorite flower at work. I followed you to make sure you were safe. I kept Danny away as much as I could."

She'd backed all the way to the door. If she wasn't cuffed, she could hide her hands behind her and open the door. Maybe she could even get it closed again before he fired off a shot.

"You were nice to me, Maggie." She was? When? "That day at the police station—after Danny tried to hurt you— you reached out to me. You touched me again that night I came to help Joe with the ants." She'd grabbed him to stop him from contaminating a crime scene. He thought that meant she cared? "Danny let the bugs out in the building, you know. He wanted a reason to come in and see you. But he won't do anything like that again."

"Let me go, Lawrence," she begged, watching the coat shrivel as it burned. "I have a child to raise. If you truly love me, you'll let me go."

"I do love you, Maggie." The bug eyes blinked and turned. "This is the only way I can keep you from ever being hurt again. This is the only way we can be together."

He dropped the coat into a puddle on the floor and the pool of chemicals exploded into toxic white-and-orange flames.

"No!" Maggie screamed and spun toward the door, but the fire raced along the floor behind her. In mere seconds, the entire door was a wall of burning wood and chemicals.

She was trapped between a killer and certain death.

"ANSWER YOUR PHONE, damn it!"

John raced through the city—his siren blaring, the lights on his truck flashing.

Twenty-four minutes without hearing a word from

Maggie. She should have called him in ten. He'd tried her cell and the apartment. Nothing.

He swung through an intersection, screeching as he careened onto the street that would take him to The Corsican. He'd already put a call in to Spencer Montgomery to warn him that Maggie might be in danger. He'd left two messages with Joe Standage, one asking when Maggie had checked in with him and another demanding that he get off his sorry butt and go find her.

Three blocks away.

He tossed the phone onto the seat beside him and gripped the wheel tighter. Driving his modified truck with his left foot was getting easier, but at this speed, even a man with control over two good feet had to be careful.

He could see The Corsican's brown facade rising above the buildings and trees.

Two blocks away. One.

"I'm comin', Sarge." *Be alive. Be strong.* "I'm comin'."

He'd promised to keep her safe. He'd promised himself.

John stomped on the brake and fishtailed around the corner, crashing through the parking garage's security gate that thus far hadn't kept out any threat to Maggie. He skidded to a stop at the base of the entrance ramp. The entire level was filled with smoke.

"Hell." He lowered his window half an inch to take a sniff of the swirling black fumes. "Ah, hell." He picked up the phone beside him and punched in 9-1-1. "This is John Murdock out of Station 23." He wheeled the truck around and sped back up the ramp to clear the entrance. "I'm reporting a fire at 11387 Mediterranean Drive—The Corsican. The basement level is engulfed with smoke. From the smell of things, it's a chemical fire. I'll begin evac."

He drove his truck around to the front of the building

and jumped out. Why the hell weren't the building alarms ringing? "Maggie!"

He grabbed a mask and helmet from the kit in the back of his truck and charged up the stairs. Inside the first-floor doors he could see the smoke, along with a toxic cloud of chemical gases, puffing up through vents and cracks. The fire had to be downstairs. Good. That meant relative containment if KCFD got here fast enough. Bad if enough air got to the source and flashover occurred. Then the whole building could light up in a matter of minutes.

If whatever chemicals those were didn't blow the place to smithereens first.

The businesslike assessment was done. His emotions were as under control as they were going to get. Time to move.

Step One—hit the alarm. Thank God. The ear-piercing honk of sound should wake even the tenants with hearing aids.

"Maggie!" Step Two—beat down Joe Standage's door and determine the worthless charmer wasn't home.

Step Three? John slipped the oxygen tank over his shoulders and shoved open the stairwell door. He was a few years and a few injuries gone from being able to sprint up the stairs like a young stud like Dean Murphy. But he intended to be at Maggie's door in a matter of seconds.

FIVE MINUTES LATER, John was working his way down from the tenth floor.

Maggie was gone. Missing. She'd never even made it to her apartment after reaching the building. He tried not to let the fear make him crazy, but this was so wrong that his heart was breaking with the thought that he was going to lose another comrade in arms. And there was no medal, no therapy that could ever heal the wound of losing the woman he loved.

Ladder trucks and hoses were positioning themselves outside. Reinforcements were already in the building, clearing tenants from the lower floors. Because he was already on the upper floors, he'd agreed to go door to door to check for elderly residents who might still be in their apartments. He intended to open every damn door in the building to find the one Maggie was hidden behind.

The Wongs were on their way down the stairs. He'd just gotten Mr. Cutlass and his cat out of their apartment. Now he was pounding on Miss Applebaum's door. He could hear the sounds of a television inside.

"Miss Applebaum!" She had about ten seconds before he busted down the door. "John Murdock here. There's a fire in the building. You have to evacuate."

Five. Four. Three. Two…

The door swung open to Joe Standage struggling to pull his pants up over his briefs. "Come on, Frances. We have to go."

John glanced beyond the half-dressed super to see his elderly neighbor pulling a bathrobe on over her nightgown. These two were in flagrante delicto? "Seriously?"

Miss Applebaum buttoned her robe right up to the neck as she stepped into the hallway. "Joe was just fixing my faucet."

Right. So all the breakdowns and seeming incompetence that required so many repairs was just a cover for an affair? So no one had really been watching over the building. No one had taken responsibility for keeping Maggie and Travis safe. Not until the day he'd moved in.

John might have laughed if the situation wasn't so dire. He grabbed the older man by the arm on his way past him. "Did you see Maggie? Did she get home all right?"

But he already knew Joe's answer. "I've been up here most of the afternoon. But I never heard anything across the hall. The elevator was having fits, though. I was gettin' set to go check it when it started running again. Went all the way down to the basement and stopped as far as I could tell. I'm gonna have to call the repair company again."

The elevator. Maggie's worst nightmare.

John hurried the older man along to the stairs with him, then passed him by. "Get Miss Applebaum outside to safety. There should be firefighters coming up the stairs to meet you."

"Where are you going?" Joe hollered after him.

Into the heart of the fire.

One way or another, he was going to find her.

He just prayed it was the right way.

MAGGIE DROPPED THE BALL bat she'd knocked Lawrence Boyle over the head with and got onto her knees beside him. Thank God her son had been a fan all his life and she'd been too sentimental to get rid of any of his equipment.

The dwindling oxygen in the storage space had made her kidnapper light-headed and disoriented anyway. So sneaking into the storage unit behind him had been more about keeping her own senses awake and sharp than about out-muscling the bug man.

She dug into the pockets of his coveralls, searching for her gun. The key to her handcuffs was still in Danny's pocket on the other side of the fire, so it was awkward to pull her battered body along the floor toward the area's lone window.

She put her nose right next to the concrete and tried to catch a breath. The flames had burned through Boyle's chemicals, but they'd burned long enough that the wood-framed doors of each unit were now burning. The ceiling was charred and black with the flames from the walls.

Maggie was roasting like a marshmallow over an open flame. The heat was cooking her skin. The smoke was stealing the breath from her lungs. The toxins in the air were stealing the life from her body.

She'd been a victim of violent love, of obsessive love. But she wasn't done with love yet. If Travis was her heart, then John Murdock was her soul. The fates couldn't be so cruel as to deny her the chance at happiness she'd so recently discovered. Her own will wouldn't allow love to be taken from her now that she'd finally found it.

Maggie dragged the gun along the concrete floor. She thought she could hear a siren outside. She'd even imagined she heard someone shouting her name. But she was so tired. Her lungs ached.

Breathe, Maggie. Fight. Live. Love John.

"Some things are worth fighting for." She whispered the mantra against the floor and then summoned the strength to push up to her knees. "*I'm* worth fighting for."

She raised the gun into the smoke and fired blindly toward the window. Her shots pinged and crashed off wood and concrete. And then she heard the explosion of shattering glass.

Oxygen rushed in as the flames licked across the ceiling. She had to get out. She had to crawl, move. Now. Before that escape route was blocked, as well.

"Maggie!"

She hadn't imagined her name.

"John?" she croaked. Her throat was so sore, her lungs so full. She coughed and stumbled to the floor.

More glass shattered. "Maggie!"

She pushed to her feet and lurched against the wall. "John?"

"Come on, Sarge. I've got you. Reach!"

Maggie clawed her way up the wall, extended her hand. "John?"

Big, gloved hands reached in through the broken window and latched on to her wrist. The hands pulled her outside and lifted her into strong arms.

"Sarge?" Definitely John's voice. "I need a medic over here! She's bleeding!" And then she was lying down on the ground. Fingers stroked across her cheek. Someone cursed. "Sarge, sweetheart, talk to me. Medic!"

Maggie faded out for a few seconds until urgent hands put a mask over her face and cool, pure oxygen streamed into her nose and mouth. She blinked her eyes open to see The Corsican's dull brown bulk towering in the distance. Bright yellow-and-white flames danced back and forth with the shower of water shooting up from the ground. Lights on bright yellow fire engines flashed on and off in her peripheral vision.

And she saw beautiful green-gold eyes watching over her with such intensity that it made her smile.

"That's it, Sarge." She was aware of the hand holding hers now, and of other hands, packing a bandage over the wound in her head. "You stay with me."

Despite the protests of the paramedic working on her, Maggie reached up to pull her oxygen mask down to her chin. "Travis?" she asked.

"He's safe," John assured her. "Detective Fensom picked him up and is driving him here now. Danny?" he asked.

"Dead. Lawrence Boyle, too, I expect."

"Boyle? The bug guy?"

"It's a long story. But not all the things that have happened were Danny's doing." She touched the bump on her forehead and winced. "Although he did do this to me."

"He's lucky he's dead, then."

She wondered if she would ever regret that Danny had been murdered. She didn't yet. "Boyle shot Danny to *save* me. Seems all of Danny's talk about me over the years got Lawrence to thinking I was some kind of ideal woman he wanted to take care of. He started the fire because he loved me."

"How is that taking care of you? That fire damn near got you killed. Forget it. Just tell it to the cops when they get here."

She nodded, happy, for now, to save enough strength so that she could turn her hand inside John's and lace their fingers together in that way that had always made her feel close to him. "And John?"

"Yeah?"

"I've decided to move out of this death trap. I can't live here. I can't be your neighbor anymore." There had to be a safer, happier, friendlier place to live somewhere in Kansas City.

The paramedic mentioned something about stitches, but John shooed him away for a few minutes. "How about moving in with me? I'm dumping this place, too. It tried to take you from me too many times—in too many ways. I'm thinking about buying a house, investing in something more permanent."

Maggie's heart jumped at the idea of being with John. But she'd acted impulsively with her heart once before and had paid dearly for it. She needed to think about this step. She pushed herself up to a sitting position on the blanket where she'd been lying. She could see now that John was wearing a firefighter's coat, and that his skin was as smudged and dirty as she suspected her own face was. He'd come for her the moment she hadn't called. He'd been there for her just like he'd promised. He'd saved her.

"I have Travis. I can't just move in with you."

He scooted closer so that his damaged leg was propped up behind her back, supporting her. "I don't like having even a thin bedroom wall between us. I want a family. I want a future. I want you. I love you."

She'd thought about it long enough.

Maggie's heart thumped loudly in her chest. She reached inside John's coat to splay her fingers over his heart and feel its strength beating in time with hers. "I love you."

Tunneling his fingers into the loose hair at her nape, John dipped his head and covered her mouth in a deep, thorough kiss. Maggie wound her arm around his neck, pulling him close and answering with all her heart.

A ten-year-old's honest voice intruded. "Eeuw."

With a laugh, John pulled Travis onto his knees beside them. "This is what you wanted, wasn't it? The three of us together as a family? Isn't that why you called me at the fire station that night?"

"I guess." Nick Fensom politely faded into the crowd and let the reunion unfold. Travis squinched up his face as Maggie pulled him into her lap and John swallowed both of them up in a hug. "I really just wanted you to teach me how to hit a home run."

John's green-gold eyes looked downright mischievous as he leaned in to give Maggie another kiss. "That will be the second thing on my list."

Epilogue

The man rubbed the hand sanitizer along every finger, from knuckle to tip.

The newspaper article by Gabriel Knight in the *Journal*'s weekend edition mentioned that one of the task force members out to catch the Rose Red Rapist had nearly died in a fire in her apartment building. There'd been two other casualties, as well. Two deaths that were of no importance to him tonight.

He massaged the sanitizing gel into his cuticles and beneath his nails and watched the lights go out inside Robin's Nest Floral Shop.

Even after reading through the article twice, he'd found no mention of any new developments on the task force's investigation, although the *No comment at this time* by lead detective Spencer Montgomery made him suspicious. Perhaps KCPD did have some kind of lead that they didn't want him to know about yet.

The voice in his head chimed in, just as he'd expected it would. *That's exactly why you need to turn this vehicle around and go home. It's too soon for this. It isn't safe.*

But he wanted, he hungered.

The young woman with short black hair, styled in those sculpted waves that meant she had enough money to go to a salon on a regular basis, came outside and locked the door. She glanced up and down the sidewalk, no doubt concerned for her safety at this time of night. She pulled down the security bars over the front window and doors and locked it, as well.

And then she looked again. Not for lurking danger. She was looking for someone in particular. Someone who hadn't shown up when they were supposed to.

The man stowed the sanitizer in his pocket and sat up behind the wheel, suddenly interested in the young shop-keeper's plight.

It's too soon. You'd be smarter to wait.

She'd made him wait. And then she'd humiliated him. They were all laughing at him.

He needed her to pay. He needed the laughter to stop.

The dark-haired woman was on her phone now, lam-basting someone as she marched up the street. Good money said the person who'd just stood her up was getting an earful.

Was she heading home? Going to the bar around the corner? Meeting someone else?

Whatever her destination, he could guess it wasn't to meet the missing friend. No, this one was too independent to go home and cry or miss out on the fun just because she was alone.

After slipping on a pair of latex gloves from his bag, he fingered the red rose he'd bought earlier today. The rose he'd bought from her at that very shop.

Don't do it. You have nothing left to prove.

Oh, but he did.

With the voice silenced and the decision made, he started the engine and pulled onto the street, following her into the night.

* * * * *

Look for KANSAS CITY COWBOY,
the next installment in Julie Miller's
thrilling new miniseries,
THE PRECINCT: TASK FORCE
coming in August 2012 only from Harlequin Intrigue

SUSPENSE

Harlequin®
INTRIGUE®

COMING NEXT MONTH
AVAILABLE JUNE 12, 2012

#1353 WRANGLED
Whitehorse, Montana: Chisholm Cattle Company
B.J. Daniels

#1354 HIGH NOON
Colby, TX
Debra Webb

#1355 EYEWITNESS
Guardians of Coral Cove
Carol Ericson

#1356 DEATH OF A BEAUTY QUEEN
The Delancey Dynasty
Mallory Kane

#1357 THUNDER HORSE HERITAGE
Elle James

#1358 SPY HARD
Dana Marton

REQUEST YOUR FREE BOOKS!
2 FREE NOVELS PLUS 2 FREE GIFTS!

♦️ Harlequin®

INTRIGUE®

BREATHTAKING ROMANTIC SUSPENSE

HII1B

Harlequin® Romantic Suspense presents the final book in the gripping PERFECT, WYOMING *miniseries from best-loved veteran series author Carla Cassidy*

Witness as mercenary Micah Grayson and cult escapee Olivia Conner join forces to save a little boy and to take down a monster, while desire explodes between them....

Read on for an excerpt from
MERCENARY'S PERFECT MISSION

Available June 2012 from Harlequin® Romantic Suspense.

"I won't tell," she exclaimed fervently. "Please don't hurt me. I swear I won't tell anyone what I saw. Just let me have my other son and we'll go far away from here. I'll never speak your name again." Her voice cracked as she focused on his gun and he realized she believed he was Samuel.

Certainly it was dark enough that it would be easy for anyone to mistake him for his brother. When the brothers were together it was easy to see the subtle differences between them. Micah's face was slightly thinner, his features more chiseled than those of his brother.

At the moment Micah knew Samuel kept his hair cut neat and tidy, while Micah's long hair was tied back. He reached up and pulled the rawhide strip, allowing his hair to fall from its binding.

The woman gasped once again. "You aren't him...but you look like him. Who are you?" Her voice still held fear as she dropped the stick and protectively clutched the baby closer to her chest.

"Who are you?" he countered. He wasn't about to be taken in by a pale-haired angel with big green eyes in this evil place where angels probably couldn't exist.

"I'm Olivia Conner, and this is my son Sam." Tears filled her eyes. "I have another son, but he's still in town. I couldn't get to him before I ran away. I've heard rumors that there was a safe house somewhere, but I've been in the woods for two days and I can't find it."

Micah was unmoved by her tears and by her story. He knew how devious his brother could be, and Micah would do everything possible to protect the location of the safe house. There was only one way to know for sure if she was one of Samuel's "devotees."

Will Olivia be able to get her son back from the clutches of evil? Or will Micah's maniacal twin put an end to them all? Find out in the shocking conclusion to the **PERFECT, WYOMING** *miniseries.*

MERCENARY'S PERFECT MISSION
Available June 2012, only from
Harlequin® Romantic Suspense, wherever books are sold.